D1565894

Free Throw

Jacqueline Guest

James Lorimer & Company Ltd., Publishers
Toronto, 1999

© 1999 Jacqueline Guest

First publication in the United States, 1999

James Lorimer & Company Ltd. acknowledges the support of the Department of Canadian Heritage and the Ontario Arts Council in the development of writing and publishing in Canada. We acknowledge the support of the Canada Council for the Arts for our publishing program.

The author would like to acknowledge the help of the Alberta Foundation for the Arts for their assistance with this project. Thank you for your support. The author would also like to thank her cyber-coach Pointman 21, a.k.a. Eric Threatt, who took time out from his studies to help her get it right. Thanks Eric! May your life be a constant series of successful three-point shots!

Cover illustration: Sharif Tarabay   Canadä

Cataloguing in Publication Data

Guest, Jacqueline
  Free throw
(Sports series)
ISBN 1-55028-665-X (bound)   ISBN 1-55028-664-1 (pbk.)

I. Title. II. Series: Sports series (Toronto, Ont.)
PS8563.U365F73 1999 C813'.54 C99-930329-5
PX7.G83Fr 1999

James Lorimer & Company Ltd.,
Publishers
35 Britain Street
Toronto, Ontario
M5A 1R7

Distributed in the United States by:
Orca Book Publishers
P.O. Box 468
Custer, Washington
98240–0468

Printed and bound in Canada.

Contents

*For my husband Gordon whose love opened a door
to a magic place where dreams come true*

1

Sometimes Life Hands You a Personal Foul

The basketball court stretched in front of him like an enormous hardwood runway and he, Matthew Eagletail, was a Canadian Snowbird pilot — outmanoeuvring and out-flying everyone on the court. Matt smiled to himself. This was as good as it gets.

He played point guard for the Tsuu T'ina School Warriors and today, his team was on fire. They were in the closing minutes of the fourth quarter and were leading their rivals, the Collingwood Cougars, by an impressive 58-30. Every guy on the team was having a great day, but Matt was having a phenomenal day!

"Jimmy, heads up!" Matt called to the Warriors' forward. Matt could see what was coming.

"Got it!" Jimmy Big Bear, their small forward, called as he intercepted a really sloppy bounce pass then, with a quick deke and dodge, started dribbling toward the Cougars' basket.

There was a lot of traffic ahead of Jimmy. Matt blasted down court to try and run some interference. Jimmy had a wicked jump shot, but would need a split second to set up. Matt was going to try and give him that split second.

As the shortest player on the team, a star basketball player wasn't the first thing you saw when you looked at Matt. In fact, he didn't look like he should be playing basketball at all. Besides being short, he wasn't overly muscular nor did he have that fluid, athletic movement that some of the other guys had. He looked more like he should be on the debating team, not one of the best basketball teams in the league.

It was only when he got on the court that it became obvious why he not only played, but was also captain of the team. He was so fast and agile, no one could keep up with him. He also had an uncanny way of anticipating the opponents' next move, so he could direct his teammates and chop the other guys' play up before it happened.

"Hustle, hustle," he called to the other Warriors, knowing Jimmy was going to try his famous jump shot as soon as he got within shooting range.

However, the real secret of Matt's success and his best talent was what had earned him the nickname *Cloud Leaper*. When it came to jumping, his legs were positively spring loaded. He'd been able to beat much taller players on tip-offs because they'd take one look at him, decide he was no threat, and be blown away when he'd out-jump them.

Matt saw the guy covering Jimmy closing in as they rushed down court. Tony Manyponies, who played power forward for the Warriors, and Mark Fox, who played shooting guard, were positioning themselves under the basket, anticipating the rebound should Jimmy's shot miss.

Without even thinking about it, Matt moved in front of the defensive player who towered over him and set a pick, hoping they were close enough for Jimmy's shot to make it.

Out of the corner of his eye, Matt saw a huge hole open up on the opposite side of the court as the Cougars all moved to stop Jimmy's fast break.

"Jimmy, quick snap," Matt called, as Jimmy closed in on the knot of players moving toward the basket with him.

"Gottcha!" he called, understanding what Matt wanted him to do.

Matt waited exactly a quarter of a second, nodded his head at Jimmy, and then started to cut to the far side of the court and the big, undefended area. Just as Matt made his move, Jimmy grinned, snapping a crisp chest pass to him, then kept running forward. His fast forward movement momentarily threw off the tall defensive player who was waiting for him and the ball.

Matt felt like his legs could carry him anywhere, do anything, fly! He drove in to the Cougars' basket. He knew as soon as he jumped that it was going to be good. He felt it. He could have sunk that basket with his eyes closed. He was that sure.

It was a perfect lay-up. *Swish.* Two more points for the Warriors!

The crowd loved it and erupted in a fresh storm of cheers and applause.

Matt looked up into the stands for his mom. She was there, like always.

"Way to go, Warriors!" she called, waving at him enthusiastically with her Warriors pennant.

He grinned and waved back.

Unfortunately, this time, she wasn't alone. Her new husband was sitting beside her. Gordon Thoreau, his new stepdad, waved at him and gave him the thumbs-up. Matt felt all his elation at a perfectly executed play evaporate. The trouble didn't stop at his stepdad. Sitting next to him was the obnoxious gaggle of geese that were his new sisters. All five of them!

The six-year-old twins, Marigold and Daisy, were dressed identically in bright pink jumpsuits with matching hair dodads. Next to them were the eight-year-old twins, Violet and

Rosemary, looking unbelievably bored and finally, twelve-year-old Jasmine — the real treat of the family.

Taking his position at the jump circle for the tip-off, Matt re-focused and concentrated on the upcoming play. The Warriors' centre, Geoff Starlight, tipped the ball to Tony Many-ponies and the team headed toward the Cougars' basket.

Matt saw the coach signalling him that there would be a substitution at the next stoppage of play. He could see José Jacobs, the sixth man, standing beside the timer's table, waiting.

When one of the Cougars was fouled out for pointlessly hacking Jimmy Big Bear, the break allowed José to enter the game. Matt was surprised when he found out he was the one going to the bench. However, he could see the coach's reasoning.

With a lead like they had, it was a good idea to let some of the other, less-played team members rack up some court time. Matt grinned at José, whose mother was Spanish and father First Nations, and jogged off the court to *ride the pine*.

Matt watched the game closely. From the bench, he was able to get a different perspective on the various plays and strategies each team used. He glanced over at the scoreboard, noting the amount of time left on the clock. He loved this gym; it was home to him. He particularly liked the way his sneakers squeaked on the special floor.

As he glanced around at the cheering fans, his eyes came to rest on his new family. His mother was really great. Her shiny black hair was cut short in a very modern style. She was in pretty good shape too, for a middle-aged lady of thirty-six, that is. She had her own successful catering business, which kept her busy a lot of the time. Matt didn't mind, because not only had she taken him with her when she could, she always got him to try any new recipes before introducing them to her clients. She would tease him that he had a future as a food critic if he couldn't be prime minister as she'd planned for him.

He watched her laughing and talking to her new husband. Her dark, copper-coloured skin seemed to glow with health and her deep brown eyes were smiling. She looked so *Indian* compared to the pale white man she sat next to. His light sandy brown hair and blue eyes made his fair skin seem even whiter compared to all the other dads in the gym.

Not that Matt disliked his new stepdad. How could he when he didn't even know the guy, not really. Matt knew he was an accountant for some big firm in Calgary. He didn't look like an accountant though. He actually looked kind of normal, like a regular dad. He always wore a fancy suit and tie to his office, but after work and on weekends, he looked like he did now, dressed in Levi's and a denim shirt, with the Nike Air sneakers that Matt had convinced him to buy. Matt had to admit that the guy had a good sense of humour and he was kind of quiet, which Matt also liked.

The worst part of the new arrangement was his five instant sisters. They ran around yelling, laughing and squawking like brightly coloured geese! The two youngest, Marigold and Daisy, had the most peculiar shade of carrot orange hair and millions of freckles. They were always giggling and whispering — a trait Matt found very annoying. They also seemed intrigued with the fact that Matt's skin was so dark and were forever asking him dumb things, such as could they see his arms or the soles of his feet to compare with theirs.

The other two twins, Violet and Rosemary, though older, weren't much better. They looked more human with short brown hair and brown eyes, but were just as annoying in another way. They were very smart and never missed an opportunity to show off to their new brother. The fact he spoke a second language, Tsuu T'ina, seemed to fascinate them. It never occurred to them that Matt had learned his native tongue before English, so, in fact, his second language was English.

They also liked to point out what they considered obvious flaws in his character, like the fact he was a boy. Matt suspected that this notion came from their older sister, Jasmine.

At twelve, Jazz was closest to him in age and, after getting to know her, he wished he was thirty, not thirteen, so he wouldn't have to have anything to do with her. She also played basketball, which should have made it easier for them to get along. It didn't.

Jazz had been the oldest in their family until her dad and Matt's mom had gotten together. She was used to being the boss, but now Matt was the oldest and, by default, had taken this title away from her. It didn't matter that he didn't want anything to do with his new sisters, let alone have to be in charge of them after school or when their parents were away. Jazz resented him for taking her place and let him know he wasn't welcome. Nothing he could say could convince her he didn't want his new title or his new life.

He watched her in the stands. Her long, straight blonde hair was pulled back in a ponytail and she wore a *Toronto Raptors* jersey. That should have been a clue right there. The Raptors! Anyone who knew anything, knew the Canadian team to beat was the Vancouver Grizzlies.

Matt glanced at the big clock at the end of the gym. The crowd began counting down the seconds ... four, three, two, one! The buzzer sounded, ending the game, and the fans roared in approval. They'd won 62-32! And Matt had scored twenty-six of those points. Not bad for a short thirteen-year-old guy, he decided, as he gathered his gear and, amid the congratulatory slaps on the back, headed for the lockers.

* * *

Matt and his new family headed to Mountain Bistro in Bragg Creek for a victory feast of first-class pizza and orange floats, Matt's favourite. Bragg Creek was a small village nestled deep in the foothills of the Rocky Mountains of Alberta. It was a friendly little town where everyone knew your name and would greet you on the street with a smile and a wave. Matt thought that for a town, it was okay. He'd been raised and still lived on the Tsuu T'ina reserve, which was situated on the rolling prairie between Bragg Creek and the city of Calgary 30 kilometres away. He liked the wide-open spaces of the reserve and the way you could get on a horse and ride for what seemed like forever. The reserve had always been his home.

Mountain Bistro was a quaint little place filled with homey accents like the quilted calico cats on the shelves and the dried wildflowers in coloured glass vases. He and his mom had been coming here for years and Matt liked the way Robin, the owner, always greeted them by name. He was used to going for pizza with just his mom. It still seemed strange to be sitting here in this crowd of people.

The two youngest twins had made headbands out of their paper placemats that said *Warriors Kick Butt*, spelt *But*. Robin was now finding a pair of scissors and tape so the girls could cut out the feathers they'd coloured and attach them to their headbands.

"Hey, Matty! Have you ever seen a real live buffalo?" Violet asked, putting the finishing touches on her bright red and yellow feather.

"Yeah, and have you ever ridden any wild ponies?" Rosemary added as she studied her yellow and red feather. The difference in the two drawings was not discernible to anyone but the twins, who assured everyone the two pictures, were, in fact, completely different.

This was what his life was going to be like, Matt thought. He glanced at his mom, who winked at him. He frowned back. She gave him a warning look.

"Actually," he began with a loud sigh so his mom would know he was doing this under duress, "there's a buffalo ranch near Bragg Creek and it's run by a white man named Mr. Olson. Maybe if you called him and asked nicely, he'd let you come up and see some *real live* buffalo. Myself, I've only seen them at the Buffalo Paddock near Banff. And as for riding wild ponies — I usually stick to the well-broken ones because they're much easier to ride." He hoped his mom appreciated the huge effort he was making. Matt glanced over at her, but she was busy colouring her own feather and seemed not to have noticed his superhuman feat.

Just then Robin arrived with the tape and scissors and the girls stopped asking him annoying questions and concentrated on positioning their feathers in exactly the right spot on the paper headbands.

Finally the pizzas arrived and, much to Matt's relief, both sets of twins eagerly began eating, diverting them from any further questions.

"It really was a great game," Matt's new stepdad said, smiling. "You were fantastic." He shovelled a huge piece of pizza onto Matt's plate.

"Thanks, ah ..." he still didn't know what to call this guy. *Dad* was out, but *Mr. Thoreau* seemed just a little formal. "Thanks," he finished lamely and took a bite of his pizza.

"You really did a good job, Honey Bear," his mom said, using her nickname for him and forgetting he'd asked her not to use mushy language in front of the new family because it embarrassed him. He shot her a glance, frowning.

She realized what she'd done, and mouthed the word "sorry."

"I got lucky," he said. "The other guys played great today too. In fact" — he paused to take another huge bite of his pizza — "we all played like NBA stars. Anyone of us could have passed for Michael Jordan, Shaquille O'Neal or Tyrone *Muggsy* Bogues," he said, smiling at the mention of the famous 5'3" NBA star. The shortest player in NBA history, Muggsy, who sported the number 1 on his jerseys, now played for the Golden State Warriors and was Matt's hero.

"You're the shrimpiest player on either team," Daisy pointed out. "Jazz said real basketball players are 8-feet high."

"Do you think you'll be 8-feet high when you grow up?" Marigold asked, a long piece of mozzarella cheese stuck to her chin.

"You never know," Matt began, trying not to sound annoyed. "Maybe, but since my mom's kinda short and my dad wasn't very tall either, the chances are pretty slim."

Matt watched, a little grossed out, as Daisy picked the cheese off Marigold's chin and threw it at Rosemary.

"Oh, yuck!" Rosemary yelled, as the cheese entangled itself in her hair. "Da-a-a-d," she wailed, dragging the word out.

"That's enough, girls," their dad said, handing Rosemary a napkin and darting a look at the two younger girls, who were giggling hysterically.

They were worse than geese, Matt thought, with their non-stop racket and their arms flapping around excitedly. He groaned inwardly. This was just plain unbelievable. How those two little monsters could be allowed in public was a mystery to him. They should be left at home with a bowl of birdseed and a stock bucket of water.

He caught Jazz watching him. She must have guessed how he felt because she tossed her pizza crust down on the plate and glared at him.

"Can we go now?" she asked in an obviously irritated tone.

"No, Jazz," her dad said. "Colleen and I have some good news." He took his wife's hand in his. "The new house is ready sooner than expected and," he said, taking a breath, "we're going to move in this weekend."

The entire table fell silent for a moment. Then all the girls started talking at once.

Marigold and Daisy wanted to go see the house again right away. Rosemary and Violet wanted to know if the painters had made their room the peach and green they'd picked out of the millions of paint chips they'd looked at.

"Quiet!" Jazz said and immediately all four of the girls stopped talking. "I thought you said it wasn't going to be ready for at least another month," she said to her dad in an accusing tone.

"I know, but we got a call earlier this week saying it was nearly ready and the finishing touches could be done while we lived in it. Isn't that great news, kids?" He looked around the table at all the faces.

"Yeah!" the younger girls all yelled. The only ones at the table who weren't smiling were Jazz and Matt.

Even though his mom and stepdad had gotten married almost a month ago, Matt and his mom had continued to live on the reserve with his grandparents just as they had since Matt's dad had been killed in a hunting accident six years ago. His mom and stepdad had bought a new home for them, but the two families couldn't move in together until the house was finished.

That wasn't supposed to be for at least another month.

Matt dreaded the thought of leaving the reserve and had spent a lot of sleepless nights trying to figure a way out of it. He'd hoped this day would never come. His home was there, with his grandparents and his friends — and his basketball team.

A terrible sinking feeling suddenly struck him.

"Mom, I know you've been looking forward to this move, but I'm right in the middle of basketball season. I can't leave the team. I'm captain, and we're going to go all the way this year. I mean the Foothills Zone Championship, that's what we've been working for. This is the first time in the three years I've been on the team that we've had a shot at the championship." He looked at his mom expectantly. She had to understand.

His mom looked momentarily uncomfortable. "Matt, I know we talked about this and I said you'd finish the year at Tsuu T'ina School. But the situation has changed. I just didn't expect everything to come together so quickly. Gordon and I weren't planning on getting married till the summer and the house, well, we didn't expect the building to go so smoothly." She reached out and took her son's hand. "Don't you see Hon … Matt. It's like we were all meant to be together. I think it's a good thing everything is working out so well." She smiled at her son. "It will take some adjusting on all our parts, but believe me, it's going to be wonderful. You'll see. We're going to make one heck of a family." She looked around the table at all the smiling faces.

"Well I think it stinks!" Jazz threw her napkin on the table. "I don't want to be one big happy family. I liked *my* family just the way it was." She pushed her chair back and stalked out of the restaurant.

"I'll go talk to her, Colleen," Jazz's father said. He glanced at the rest of the girls, who now looked very confused, and added, "It's okay girls. Jazz just needs a little time to adjust to our new life." He nodded at his wife and went after his oldest daughter.

"Don't worry, girls," Matt's mom said, smiling at each of the girls in turn. "I'm sure once we're settled into our new house, we'll all get used to our new life and our new family." She nodded reassuringly at them. "Remember, we're not moving far from where you live now. In fact, lots of things will stay the same. You'll have your old post office box, your old phone number, and you'll even ride the same school bus to Bragg Creek School."

The girls seemed to be calming down.

"And I'll come and visit every weekend," Matt added casually.

His mother looked at him quizzically. "What do you mean, Matthew?" she asked.

"Mom, I've thought about this and I don't want to leave the reserve. I'm going to stay living with Grandpa and Grandma. It's my home." Matt could feel his heart pounding. He knew this was not what his mother wanted and the timing was way off, but he had to make a stand. He couldn't leave his home, his friends, and certainly not his basketball team.

As soon as she started to speak, Matt knew he'd made a mistake.

"What are you talking about, Matt? Of course you'll be living with me and your new family," she said in a brusque tone. She saw the look on Matt's face and her voice softened. "I'm sorry, Honey Bear, but if this family is going to make it, we have to stick together. On Monday, you'll be enrolled at Bragg Creek School. I've already talked to your teachers at Tsuu T'ina School. They said they will miss you, but wish you well in your new life."

Matt listened to her words in disbelief. "You already talked to my teachers? When?"

"This afternoon, before the game. I wanted to tell you sooner, but we decided to wait and tell everyone at the same time. This all happened so quickly. I know it seems hard now, dear, but if this is going to work, we all have to give a 100 percent." Matt heard another tone in her voice he'd come to know. It was the one she used when her mind was absolutely made up, the one that meant there'd be no compromise.

"But Mom, the team ..." he began.

"No, Matt. This is not open for discussion. We're starting a new life and we're starting it together." She reached out to touch his hair. "Trust me, this is going to work."

Matt couldn't believe what he was hearing. He knew one day his mom would move in with her new husband and the Geese, but he'd always secretly thought he'd just stay living with his grandparents, like always. In his mind, he'd never accepted it really happening. He thought his mom would understand that some things were more important — like basketball.

He could feel his world starting to crack apart and he felt helpless to stop it.

2

A Personal Foul Gets You a Free Throw

Jeez, can you move a little faster?" Jazz grumbled irritably. Protectively clutching a small cardboard box in her arms, she shoved violently past Matt, who was just about to start up the main stairs of their new house.

The two large boxes he had stacked one on top of the other, teetered precariously in his grasp.

"Hey, watch it!" he yelled, hastily setting the two boxes on the floor. The weekend was here and they were moving into the new family house, like it or not. For Matt, it was *not*. They'd been moving boxes all morning and Matt couldn't believe they were only about half done.

He sighed, picked up the two boxes, and again started up the stairs. Jazz, on her way back down, brushed past him, almost upsetting the boxes for the second time. "Jazz, for crying out loud, will you look where *I'm* going?" he called to her retreating back.

Ignoring him, she tossed a long blonde braid over her shoulder and kept going.

Jazz and Matt were avoiding each other as much as possible, but it was difficult when they were moving into the same house. Somehow, invisible battle lines had been drawn between them.

Matt set the two boxes down in Marigold and Daisy's room.

"Here you go girls — enjoy." Matt turned to leave the twins to unpack.

"Matty, those boxes are for Violet and Rosemary, silly!" Daisy said, eyeing the two large boxes.

"It says *Girls' Room*. You're girls ... right?" Matt asked.

"No, no, no! We're *Twins' Room*. Violet and Rosemary are *Girls' Room*. That's how daddy tells us apart." Marigold looked at him as though he was trying her patience. "Don't boys know anything?" she asked, rolling her eyes.

Matt picked up the boxes and headed for the other twins' bedroom, mumbling to himself as he went.

Walking down the wide hallway, which had boxes stacked against the walls, he thought the big sprawling house looked more like a country inn than someone's home. It had so many bedrooms, it could have been a hotel.

His mom and stepdad's large room had a fireplace and each set of twins had a big bedroom which, when they grew older, could be separated into two rooms.

Jazz had her own room, which she liked a lot. She'd shared a room with Violet and Rosemary in their old house and was thrilled with the prospect of her own walk-in closet. Matt figured that was a girl thing.

His room, and he was particularly grateful for this, was two floors down and away from all the Geese. It was in the walkout basement, where the family room was. He was the only one down there and that suited him fine. He even had his own small fireplace, which he was allowed to use if he followed all the safety rules. He knew about burning wood, as his grandparents always kept a fire going in their airtight stove. In fact, for a long time, his grandma had refused to get rid of her wood-burning stove when they'd modernized the farm.

A unique feature of the new, spacious house was a hidden second set of narrow stairs that ran the entire height of the three-story house. The twins called it the *secret passage*.

It was handy for taking boxes down to the garage or the construction shed, where they were storing the stuff they didn't know what to do with yet. The shed was out behind the garage and you could get to it by an outside access door beside Matt's room. The outside entrance would be cool when he got older. He could come in late and not disturb the whole house. This little detail would drive the Geese crazy. He liked the idea of their not knowing when he came and went.

He'd just put an armful of clothes in his room and was starting back up the hidden stairs, when he ran smack into Jazz, who was coming down with a large box destined for the construction shed. This time, however, Matt stood his ground. No more Mr. Nice Guy.

"Oomph!" she gurgled as she fell over with the box landing awkwardly on top of her.

She struggled with the box for a minute, then lay still under it.

"Are you just going to stand there gawking or are you going to help?" she asked, her voice muffled. She'd fallen backward into the narrow access to the stairs and the box was wedged in the entryway.

Matt looked at her legs sticking out from under the huge box and something about it struck him as funny. It could have been because Jazz's voice seemed to be emanating from a big, brightly coloured picture of a cow's head Marigold and Daisy had drawn on the outside of the box.

He couldn't help it. He started laughing. It just looked so ridiculous. This smiling cow's head with girl legs, stuck in the stairway, flailing about like a freshly caught trout in the bottom of a boat.

Unfortunately, Jazz couldn't see the humour in the situation.

"Get this box off me right now you big, dumb ...."

There was a pause and Matt suddenly stopped laughing. Big, dumb what? He'd heard comments like this before, usually from people who didn't like him just because he was Indian.

His stomach tensed.

"*BOY!*" she yelled loudly, kicking futilely at the box.

Now *that* was funny! He broke out into a fresh round of laughter. True, he was a boy, but he sure wasn't big and he'd never considered himself dumb.

He could have gone on laughing, but in the interest of what little family harmony remained between them, he decided he'd better try to control himself as he helped his stepsister free herself.

Once on her feet again, Jazz grabbed the box and stormed past him. "You're such a nerd!" she said as she pushed out the door.

"Gee, ungrateful or what," he said, and burst out laughing again. Jazz just glared at him as she slammed the door behind her. Matt shrugged and headed up the narrow passage to the kitchen. "Girls!" he grumbled, taking the stairs two at a time.

The kitchen was huge with lots of modern gadgets. A cheerful, sunny room, Matt's mom would enjoy preparing her catering foods in the two commercial-sized stoves she'd had specially installed.

Matt glanced out one of the large windows that overlooked the garage and backyard. His stepdad had said one of the first things they were going to do was put up a basketball hoop over the garage door. He thought the large cement parking area would make a great place to play pickup.

Play? Who with, Matt had wondered, turning away from the window.

* * *

Matt leaned his arms on the veranda railing and watched the
early-morning sun climb into the perfectly blue sky. It was
quite the house, all right, and he would have thought it neat
except for one thing — he had to live in it.

He looked around. The house was situated on the side of a
hill and when he sat in the porch swing and looked to the east,
he could see the Tsuu T'ina Reserve, where his grandparents
lived. He wondered what they were doing, if Grandma had
made any fresh bannock and strawberry jam he loved so
much, how the Warriors were doing. Thinking of his team
gave him a fresh pang of what he was sure was homesickness
for the only place he really thought of as home.

On the south side of the house, he could just make out the
Bragg Creek School through the thick stands of tall evergreen
and poplar trees. It was less than two kilometres from where
they lived, but to Matt, it represented a whole other world. He
wasn't looking forward to today and his new school, but try as
he might, he hadn't been able to change his mom's mind.
She'd meant what she'd said. She intended to make this new
family work.

Matt had always admired the way his mom approached
problems with focus and confidence. When she set her mind
to something, it happened. It was as simple as that. She'd
always told him that whatever you want, you can have, as long
as you make the magic happen. The *magic* was hard work and
determination, which she had tons of.

"All set?" his mom asked, coming out onto the veranda
and startling him out of his daydream. She would take him to
school today, since he had to be officially enrolled. At least
he'd been spared riding on a packed school bus with the
Geese.

"Yeah, sure," he mumbled, looking at the tops of his sneakers. He couldn't look at her because if he did he was afraid he'd do something stupid, like start crying. He still felt like he was in a bad dream and any minute now, he'd wake up and find himself on his old school bus riding to Tsuu T'ina School with all his friends.

He didn't wake up.

* * *

Bragg Creek Elementary and Junior High, Bragg Creek School for short, was a nice enough school, as strange schools go, he thought as he listened to his new math teacher finish telling them what their homework assignment was.

He'd made it through his first day, barely. The kids had all been extra polite, which was kind of insulting. They really knew how to make a guy feel like an outsider. But Matt decided he really didn't mind that. He didn't want to fit in here. He didn't want to get to know these kids or find out their names. He wanted to go back to his old school. Today was Monday and after school, the Warriors would be having a practice. He should be there.

To make matters worse, as the new *older brother*, he was expected to stay after school and wait for Jazz to finish her basketball practice, so they could walk home together through the big, bad woods. Like anything would mess with a girl like Jazz! He pitied the poor bear that crossed paths with his new stepsister.

The thought of basketball made his throat suddenly feel tight. He'd called all his buddies from the Warriors and told them his bad news. They were as choked as he was. He'd told them he hadn't given up yet and he'd continue to try and find a way to get back to Tsuu T'ina School. In the meantime, he'd try to make it for a game of pickup, maybe on the weekend.

"Come on, Matt, I'm going to be late," Jazz said, as they walked side by side on their way to the gym. "Mom said you've got to baby-sit me, so *baby-sit!*" She slammed through the gym doors and went to drop her bag of stuff by the bench. "The Bandits are coming in right after our practice, so I don't want to waste any time waiting for you." She waved a friendly hello to the assembled girls waiting for her.

The Bragg Creek Bandits, Matt knew, was the school's top-ranked basketball team. Tsuu T'ina had played them a couple of times, one win, one loss. Matt remembered some of the team members. Serious guys when it came to the game, which was how it should be.

"You can wait in the stands over there," Jazz said dismissively, pointing to the bleachers on the far side of the court.

"I know," he said, ignoring her tone and moving toward the seats.

This place didn't even smell like a gym. In fact, it had an odd kind of antiseptic odour.

Matt settled down to watch his stepsister's team go through its practice. The team was divided into two squads, setting up for a man-to-man defence.

Coach Blande blew the whistle and the two teams formed up at the centre circle. Jazz was a kind of player coach. She watched the girls play and helped out with the weak areas, which, Matt thought, were many. He watched her play and had to admit that she was pretty good. She also gave the other girls the right advice as they moved through the drills. She could see their weaknesses and zeroed in on them mercilessly. Jazz was no mother hen.

As he watched, he noticed a lot of problems, like passing skills and ball control. Their passes were slow and sloppy. They'd be picked off easily. Some of the girls telegraphed whom they were going to pass to so obviously, they may as well have yelled the receiver's name. And dribbling — half the girls still watched the ball, instead of where they were going. Basic skill problems, he thought, shaking his head.

Some of the younger guys at Tsuu T'ina had had the same problems. By practising some special drills, they generally improved quite quickly. If Jazz's team practised those same drills, Matt was sure things would improve. His coach had always told him that if you don't have the basics down cold, you'll never get any better, no matter how long you play.

Another thing he'd noticed really struck home. A lot of the girls were rather short. They were quick enough and seemed to be able to control where they went, but their height seemed to be an obstacle that they couldn't overcome. Matt knew just how to use his size to his advantage and these girls could easily do the same. Sometimes, you're as tall as you think you are. This team could really be something with the right information — like we don't all have to be Wilt the Stilt to be a great basketball player. If you used your head on the court, it gave you at least two inches in height advantage.

Matt took a deep breath. He and Jazz might not like each other, might not even speak to each other at home, but when it comes to *the game*, you have to put certain things aside.

He started back down toward the bench. When a break was called and the team came off the court, Matt was waiting for Jazz.

"Hey, Jazz," he began. "I was watching you play and I think I have a couple of drills that could help."

Jazz stopped dead still and just stared at him.

"Back at Tsuu T'ina, some of the younger players had the same problems your team has with ball control. I have a couple of dribbling drills that can really make a difference. What you need to do ..."

She cut him off. "What *you* need to do, *Hot Shot*, is to mind your own business. We're quite capable of solving a few dribbling problems without your interfering." Her voice had become quite loud now and the other players had stopped to watch them.

"Look, all I was trying to do was help. Your ball control stinks and your passing skills are in the toilet." His voice had gone up a couple of notches also.

She threw the towel she'd been wiping her hands with onto the bench. "You may be the new big brother at home, but here, this is my team, and we're doing just fine without some armchair gunner mouthing off. If you want to play ball so badly, the Bandits will be here in an hour. Why don't you try your cheap coaching advice on them!" Her face was red and her hands were shaking.

Matt couldn't believe how angry she'd become. Of all the ungrateful ... He turned and stamped out of the gym. He had to. His mom had taught him never to slug a girl.

He strode down the corridor, trying to walk off the anger he felt. Of all the arrogant, self-centred, know-it-all ...

He shrugged his shoulders. Fine! Her and her whole team could spend the rest of the season in the dumpster for all he cared.

He noticed a sign on the door at the end of the hall marked *Library*. Walking up to the door, he opened it and had a quick look around.

The room was bright and sunshine streamed though the large windows at one end. There were shelves of books everywhere as well as several computer terminals. This school was really different in that there were computers scattered throughout community areas for students to use whenever they wanted. The only computer he'd had any experience with was his mom's laptop she used with her catering business. He'd decided to stay away from the computers until he had a chance to figure out how they worked. He didn't want to look dumb in front of his new classmates.

There were a couple of kids still working on the softly humming machines. Matt walked over to watch.

One of the guys looked up as he moved behind him. He was a slim, dark-haired boy with a hawklike nose that made him look strong and confident.

"Hi, I'm yakking with a buddy of mine in Australia. We're discussing whether the Great Barrier Reef is dying off from pollution or just going through a natural phase." He went back to watching the lines appearing on the screen. "There's a couple of other kids coming in to our chat room now. See, each sentence starts with the name of the person who wrote it."

Matt watched, forgetting his anger at his stepsister, fascinated by the rolling lines on the screen in front of him.

"This is great! How did you find this guy?" Matt asked.

"Oh, I just got into this natural science chat room and asked if anyone wanted to talk about the Great Barrier Reef. Poof! Twenty people jumped in." He laughed warmly. "It's easy, give it a try." He motioned to one of the other empty terminals.

Matt shook his head. "Ah ... I've never done any computer stuff. I don't think I ..."

"That's crazy talk, man," the friendly student said, smiling at Matt. "Just get on the Net and go to the chat room of your choice. There's hundreds of them." He noticed Matt's blank look. "A chat room is a place where you can have a real-time conversation with someone by typing in a sentence, which he reads instantly and then answers you right back. It's like talking with type." He quickly typed something in, then got up and motioned for Matt to sit down at the next terminal.

He nodded at his machine. "I said I had to leave the room for a couple of minutes, but would be back. My name's Collin, and I'll be your tour guide today." He laughed and pointed to the keyboard on Matt's computer. "Okay, just follow my instructions and I'll walk you through."

Collin showed him how to log on and sign up to use a chat room. When it came to a cyber-name, Matt was at a loss.

"What interests you? Pick something that goes with that," Collin advised. "Take me, I go by the handle *Hat Trick* because I'm into hockey. Don't be shy. That's the beauty of the Web — no one suspects you're a geeky thirteen-year-old nerd. For all they know, you're a sophisticated, fourteen-year-old man of the world." He laughed. "Got to get back to *Great White*, my mate from down under," he said, affecting an Australian accent. "Just let me know if you have any problems."

He smiled at Matt and left for his own terminal.

Matt watched him go. This guy was okay.

Matt thought for a moment. He knew what his cyber-name would be: Point Guard. Collin was right. It was something he was into. It was a natural. Following the instructions he'd been given, Matt typed in his cyber-ID and, zap, he was surfing the Web! He decided it might be cool to go to a chat room and talk about ... basketball. He smiled to himself and hit NBA chat.

The screen came to life with lines of comments people in the chat room were making. Each person's cyber-name and comment were in a different colour, which made it easy to tell who was speaking. He read the comments focusing on whether the Bulls were going to beat the Pacers for top spot in the Central Division. Now this was something he understood.

Point Guard signed on with a small comment on the superiority of the Utah Jazz.

All of a sudden, he had all kinds of comments tossed back at him on the fact that the Jazz were in the Midwest Division and they were good but ... For the next half-hour Matt chatted about his favourite players, teams and stats. One guy, who went by the name *Free Throw*, really knew his stuff. He and Matt had pretty well dissected all four divisions and Matt was really getting the hang of this chat room stuff when Free Throw sent him a message that reminded him he was new to cyberspace.

Free Throw: Point Guard, why don't we PM so these cheeseballs can't interrupt?

Matt just stared at the screen. Now what?

"Collin, can I ask you a dumb question?" He looked over at the guy busy typing at the next terminal.

"No such thing as a dumb question, old buddy, just dumb answers. What's up?" Collin asked, still typing.

"This guy wants me to *PM*, but I don't know what that means." Matt sat looking at the screen, not knowing what to do.

Another message for him scrolled across the screen.

Free Throw: Hey, Point Guard, you still there?

Matt just sat there, unsure what to do.

Collin stopped typing for a moment. "He wants to *private message* you. Just click on his name and hit the PM button at the bottom. It makes it much easier to have a serious conversation." He went back to his keyboard.

Matt did as he was instructed and the screen changed. Another message box came up, this one addressed to Free Throw. Matt typed in *hello*, and hit enter.

That's all it took.

Free Throw and Matt started chatting like they were old friends. They decided on whom they'd pick for their own dream teams, who'd coach and who deserved the highest salary.

Matt completely lost track of the time. This was great! Free Throw was really something.

"So this is where you've been hiding out! Do you know I've been standing at the front doors for twenty minutes?"

Jazz's irritated voice cut threw Matt's concentration. He looked up at his furious stepsister, then at his watch.

"Oh, hey, I lost track of time. Just a minute." He quickly typed a message.

Point Guard: Hey, Free Throw, Buddy — my jock of a stepsister is finished her b-ball practice and I've got to go. I'll talk to you tomorrow. Same room, same time.

Free Throw: Your sister plays b-ball? Okay! Must be nice having someone in the family you can shoot hoops with.

Matt looked at this last message.

Point Guard: Shoot hoops with Jazz? LOL!!!!

He disconnected from the server and shut the computer down.

Jazz stood at the door to the library, her knapsack swinging impatiently.

"Look, I'm sorry. I was really enjoying using the Internet and I just lost track of time. Haven't you ever done anything so normal?" he asked, hurrying to catch up with her as she headed down the hallway.

"Jerk!" she retorted, and tossed her ponytail with a superior air.

"Snappy comeback, Jazz," Matt said just as sarcastically, pushing open the outside doors.

They walked along together in silence as they headed for home. Matt would haved liked to tell someone about his experience on the Net and meeting Free Throw. Someone, but not Jazz. He didn't want anything to do with her unless he absolutely had to.

They cut through a heavily wooded area and started following an old animal track that would take them to the edge of their property. The late afternoon sun slanted through the new green poplar leaves, giving the path an eerie greenish light.

A sudden rustling from the underbrush up ahead made Matt stop.

"What's the matter now, Hot Shot, tired?" Jazz said, starting to push past him.

Matt grabbed her arm and pulled her behind him.

"Hey! Watch it, that hurt." She rubbed her arm.

"Shh!" Matt admonished, still trying to pinpoint where the noise had come from.

Jazz stopped rubbing her arm and looked around. "What?" she asked, irritated, but Matt noticed she'd lowered her voice.

"I heard something in the trees. Probably just a deer, but ..." He let the sentence hang.

"But it could be a bear or cougar, you mean?" she asked, peering into the dense foliage, trying to spot whatever Matt had heard.

Matt looked for a stick to use for a weapon.

A twig snapping behind them made both of them whirl around.

"Jazz, when I say run, you run!" he whispered to her, holding the stick out in front of him like some medieval knight's lance.

The bushes in front of him moved.

"Run!" he yelled at his stepsister.

3

New Player

Matt tried to swallow, but his throat was dry. He tightened his grip on the stick he was holding.

Then he heard it — a low, ominous growling. Taking a deep breath, Matt readied himself.

The bushes directly in front of him started to move.

Suddenly, from between the leafy green bushes, out poked the head of a big, white dog with sad, dark eyes and very large teeth.

Matt exhaled the breath he hadn't realized he'd been holding and lowered his stick, just a little. A stray dog he could probably handle.

"Hello, boy. Did we scare you?" He smiled at the dog, being careful not to show any teeth, which the dog might interpret as an aggressive sign. "Because you sure as heck scared us!"

Jazz came up behind him. "Oh, Matt, look how cute he is," she gushed and pushed past him to get a better look at the dog.

"Jazz, wait a minute," he warned, raising the stick again and holding it between Jazz and the mutt. "That's a 150-pound stray dog that just growled at me. We better make sure what his intentions are before we get too friendly."

"Don't be silly. Look at him. He's a big, furry sweet-heart." She shoved his stick out of the way as if to dismiss any worries about the dog's intent, and started toward the animal.

"Hello, boy. Are you lost? Where do you live? Did you lose your mommy and daddy?" she asked the large dog in a singsong, baby-talk voice. The dog was now snuffling her hand and waving his huge, plumed tail.

Matt couldn't believe what he was hearing. *Mommy and daddy?*

"Come on, Jazz. Leave the mutt alone." Matt tossed his stick down. "He's probably just run away from some rancher and will go home if you stop talking to him like an idiot."

"Don't you listen to that smart-aleck Hot Shot, Precious. Are you thirsty, boy? It's so hot out today." Jazz went on talking to the dog, ignoring Matt's advice. "Come on, I'll get you a nice drink of cool well water. Come on, Precious." She patted her leg and started along the path toward home.

Matt couldn't believe the way his stepsister was acting. He'd never seen this side of her. And this side was truly weird!

All the way home, Jazz talked to the stray, who seemed to enjoy the sound of her voice as he trotted at her side. It couldn't be, but the dog actually seemed to be understanding what she said.

Matt followed behind, knowing he couldn't stop Jazz if he wanted to.

When they got home, Jazz got the dog a large bucket of water and let him drink his fill.

"You shouldn't encourage him, Jazz. He has a home somewhere, just let him get back to it."

Jazz studied the dog. "I don't think so. Look at how matted and dirty his coat is." She ran her hands down the sides of the dog. "Oh, Matt, feel how skinny he is. He's starving. If he does belong to someone, they should be ashamed for treating him like this."

"I'm not touching that shaggy beast. He's probably got fleas," Matt said, shaking his head.

Jazz's hands involuntarily pulled back from the dog's mangy coat for just a second. Then she continued checking the dog over. "That's all you know, Hot Shot. There are no fleas here. It's too high and too cold in Bragg Creek for the little pests."

Matt just continued shaking his head as he started inside. "Suit yourself, but I suggest you send him on his way before Mom and ..." He still didn't know what to call his new stepdad. "Before Mom and your dad get home."

When he left, Jazz was still goo-goo talking to the big dog. He sat with his alert, black-rimmed eyes watching her and listening intently to every word.

* * *

At dinner, when questioned about the dog, Jazz casually shrugged her shoulders and said he was gone. She said he'd had a couple of more drinks, then headed off down the hill toward the path they'd come up on.

The discussion then turned to basketball and the after-school practice. Matt noticed how animated Jazz's voice became when she talked about her team.

"Then after practice, I waited for Matt to come to the gym like we'd arranged, but he didn't show up." She shot Matt a look that said she was enjoying this. "I figure it was because the Bandits were on the court, and Matt didn't want to watch. He's probably jealous of how well the Bandits play. He hasn't said so, but he's pining for his old team at Tsuu T'ina." She gave him a sidelong glance. "I found him in the library, *on line*. I think he has a new cyber-girlfriend. He was sure typing like he was in love."

Violet and Rosemary giggled and Marigold and Daisy started chanting, "Matty has a girlfriend! Matty has a girlfriend!"

If he'd been close enough, he would have kicked Jazz under the table. As it was, his mom raised an eyebrow, questioningly.

"Well, that *is* news." She smiled warmly at her son. "I didn't know you were such an expert on The World Wide Web, Matt. Tell us about it." She took a hot roll out of a small, wicker-woven basket, then passed the basket to Violet.

Matt felt his face grow hot. Somehow, he'd get Jazz for this. "Actually, it was my first time in a chat room. This guy at school showed me how and I thought I'd try. Once I logged on, I went to a basketball room and started having this conversation with this really neat guy. He calls himself Free Throw, that's the name he uses when he's on line," he explained to Marigold and Daisy.

"You mean like his secret agent name so you don't know who he is?" Daisy asked, her big blue eyes wide with interest.

"Yeah, that's right." Matt had forgotten his embarrassment and was now excitedly talking about his new-found friend. "He knows lots about the game. We both plan on being in the NBA when we get older. We discussed players and teams, coaches, everything ... it was great!" He reached for the basket of rolls.

"Speaking of teams, have you thought about playing for the Bandits? I hear they're a topnotch squad and could probably use a player of your calibre," his stepdad asked, looking at him expectantly. "And while we're on the subject, I guess you haven't been out to the garage yet?"

He smiled at Matt, but at the mention of playing for the Bandits, Matt had immediately stopped feeling great. The idea made his stomach flip-flop. It was out of the question. He was a Tsuu T'ina Warrior, he always had been and he always would be.

"Actually, I'm through eating. May I be excused?" He looked at his mom.

She could see he was upset. "Sure, honey. The girls can do the dishes tonight."

Matt started down to his room feeling worse than he'd felt all day. The thought of playing for another team was hard enough to imagine, but playing for the Bandits was completely out of the question. Matt thought about what had happened last year. There was no way he was *ever* going to play for that team!

Just past his room was the door that led outside. He glanced through the window in the door and stopped in his tracks. Through the window he could see the garage and the paved area in front of it. Over the garage door, at what looked exactly 10 feet from the ground, was a new orange and white basketball hoop, complete with backboard and, sitting beside the garage wall, a new Spalding ball.

This was what his stepdad must have meant when he'd asked if Matt had been out to the garage! He'd been so upset, he hadn't realized what his stepdad was telling him. The idea of being able to shoot hoops at his own house was exciting. Back home, on his grandparents' farm, he'd had nothing like this.

Forgetting his bad mood, Matt headed out to test the new setup.

He was still practising jump shots late into the evening when the yard light, which was on a motion sensor, clicked on. He knew it must be late and he also knew his mom was not bugging him about it because she'd sensed he was upset. He also knew she had figured out why. He fired one more shot at the new hoop. His stepdad had said he would put up a hoop and he had. That, Matt had to admit, was pretty cool.

* * *

He'd finally gone to bed and had felt a lot better after practising. There was something about the sound of the swish when you had nothing but net. It was the best sound in the world.

He'd just shut out his light and was settling down when he thought he heard something. He listened in the darkness, unsure what it was. Then he knew. It was someone coming down the narrow hidden stairs that led from the upper levels. He waited, listening intently.

Very slowly, careful to make no noise, someone opened the back door, then just as silently, closed it behind them.

Curious, Matt got up and put on his housecoat to go see who was sneaking around in the dark. Looking outside, he realized it was completely dark. Whoever it was, they'd thought to shut off the motion sensor light so they wouldn't be seen.

Trying not to make any noise, Matt pulled open the door and slipped out into the backyard.

He heard someone in the construction shed whispering something he couldn't quite make out. As stealthily as possible, Matt moved to the corner of the shed. He cautiously made his way around the side toward the half-open door.

He'd just eased through the door, when his foot stepped on a dry twig. Snap!

In the blink of an eye, he was being hurled back against the shed wall as something huge and white slammed into him! He heard the deep, throaty growl and saw the bared white teeth gleaming in the pale moonlight that streamed through the open door.

"Precious, stop that! It's only Hot Shot sneaking around following me." Jazz's voice came to Matt from out of the darkness.

Immediately the huge dog released him and Matt scrambled back out of the shed.

Slowly, Matt's eyes adjusted to the dim light. He could see the big, mangy stray standing in the doorway between him and Jazz, eyeing him suspiciously.

"What's he doing here? I thought you said he took off after he had a drink," Matt asked in an accusing tone as he dusted off his housecoat.

"Shh, Mom and Dad will hear you," Jazz whispered loudly. "Get in here," she ordered, motioning for him to come into the shed.

"Call Godzilla off first."

"You nerd," she hissed at Matt. "Precious, with me!" she commanded and the huge dog obediently padded over and sat beside his new master.

Once inside the small outbuilding, Matt could see a bed of old blankets made up in the corner behind a stack of boxes and a bucket of fresh water beside it. There was also an empty dish on the floor beside the bucket.

"You were feeding him! That's why he's still here. I told you not to encourage him, Jazz. What are you going to do with this big, mangy rug? You sure can't keep him."

A low growl started somewhere deep in the dog's throat. Matt noticed the dog had not taken his eyes off him and when he moved, the dog would casually shuffle around so he kept himself between Matt and Jazz.

Jazz put her hand protectively on the big dog's head. "Of course I'm feeding him. He was starving. He doesn't have a collar, or tags or tattoos. I'm telling you, he's a stray and I'm not going to abandon him. I figure once I clean him up a little, bath and brush him, you know, make him presentable, then

I'll show him to Mom and Dad. I just need a little time to …
prepare him." She stroked his back. "And if you can keep your
nosy mouth shut, everything will be okay."

"My *nosy mouth*?" Matt asked incredulously. "What the
heck is a *nosy mouth* and how do I keep it shut?" He could
feel a grin starting, but didn't want to let Jazz off the hook that
easily.

"You know perfectly well what I mean, so stop acting
dumb. Or maybe you're not acting," she added sarcastically.

"That's it! I'm out of here. Mom and your dad are going to
be interested in what's out here." He turned to go.

"Matt, wait a minute," her voice softened. "Maybe we can
work something out." She sighed defeatedly. "What do you
want to keep quiet?"

He couldn't believe what he was hearing. She wanted to
make a deal so he wouldn't squeal. This was sweet. He
wouldn't bother to tell her he wasn't really going to go running to their parents. He could let her in on that little secret
later.

He rubbed his chin and looked thoughtful. "What do I
want? Let me think …." He could see she was starting to get
angry. "Okay, here's the deal. You lay off all the nasty stuff,
like the *cyber-girlfriend* business tonight, that you've been
doing to make my life more miserable than it already is and
I'll forget I saw you and the mutt."

"Sure, I can do that" she agreed quickly.

Too quickly. Matt could see he needed more practice at
this blackmail stuff.

"And …" he dragged the word out trying to think of
something else to ask for. "You do my chores for a month," he
finished quickly, grinning mischievously at her.

Even in the dim light cast by the moonlight slanting
through the door, he could see her face getting red.

"Okay, anything else?" she asked through clenched teeth.

"No, that about does it. Boy, you must really want that dog!" He laughed and turned to leave, then stopped. "Oh, and by the way, I think the lawnmower is just about out of gas. You might want to check into that before you start to mow the lawn tomorrow."

He could hear her cursing as he made his way back to the house.

* * *

The rest of the week was almost unbearable, even with Jazz leaving him alone. It turned out Bragg Creek was a basketball-crazy school and everyone was wildly speculating about where the Bandits would end up in the standings and whether or not they would take the Zone Championship. Matt tried not to discuss it, which turned out to be easy, since he didn't encourage any of his new classmates to talk to him. Why should he try to make new friends when he had lots back at Tsuu T'ina?

Besides, if he wanted to talk b-ball, he just went on line and dialled up Free Throw. When Matt had explained what was going on, Free Throw had seemed to know exactly what to say, as if he understood what it meant to lose your special team and how it felt.

Point Guard: So you see, Free Throw, even though I love the game, it wouldn't be the same playing with anyone but the Warriors.

Free Throw: I know how you feel, like you owe your team something. But as a wise guy once said, The Game is everything. I know I couldn't give up the game if I had another chance to play, even on an old rival team, but you've got to do what you think is right for you.

Matt thought about this. Free Throw was right, he had to do what was right for him — no matter what.

4

Pushing, Blocking and Charging Aren't Always Fouls

Saturday turned out to be one of those rare late spring days when the weather hinted at the heat of summer to come.

It was already quite warm when Matt, his mom and both sets of twins climbed into the big Dodge Grand Caravan minivan. It reminded Matt of a school bus, the seats full of obnoxiously noisy geese. His mom's Chevy Astro, which was perfect for the catering business and one son, was too small to hold the newly expanded family. They were going to visit the Tsuu T'ina reserve today, where his mom would show the Geese around and let them visit with their new grandparents.

Matt planned on playing basketball with some of the Warriors. He had to hand it to Jazz; she'd stuck to her word. When his stepdad had said they were going to clean the garage today, Jazz had jumped in and *volunteered* to do it for him.

He didn't know what Jazz did with the mutt during the day, but each night he heard her sneak downstairs and out to the shed. Later, he'd hear her silently head back upstairs, accompanied by a softly padding friend.

The drive to the reserve felt like going home to Matt, which is what it was. He couldn't wait to play ball with his buddies. When his mom dropped him off at Tsuu T'ina school and the outside basketball court in the school's playground, his friends were already there, waiting for him. They greeted him like the long-lost brother he was.

They played hard, with his friends' quizzing him about his new life as they sweated in the warm sunshine. It felt great as they showed off new skills and practised old ones. Matt worked on his free throw while Jimmy practised lay-ups. Geoff had mastered the tip-in like he was wearing velvet gloves, while no one could touch Mark Fox on ball control. Every one of Matt's friends seemed to have a particular skill to add to the team. Now, Matt was no longer a part of that team and worse, he had left a hole that would be hard to fill.

Just as Matt and his friends finished playing their last game, his mom pulled up in the big van.

She waved at the other boys and waited as Matt climbed in.

"You look like you had a good time," she commented as they swung out of the parking lot and headed toward his grandparents' farm for a late lunch.

"I had a great time. Those guys are the best." He grinned at her.

It was true. They were the best and he felt better than he'd felt in quite a while.

His grandparents' farm was a small holding that ran a few head of horses and some cattle. His grandparents had sold most of their stock when his granddad's health had started failing. Now they were content with the scaled-down version of the farm.

His grandparents were thrilled to see him and the twins. Their lunch was noisy, with the Geese babbling about everything his mom had shown them that morning.

After lunch, both sets of twins went outside to explore, while his mom and grandma cleared away the dishes. His grandfather had asked Matt to help him in the barn.

"How do you like your new family," his grandfather had asked as they entered the cool dimness of the old barn. It smelled of fresh hay and oiled saddles. Matt thought it was the best smell in the world. After his dad had died, he used to come out here and lay up in the loft looking out across the fields of rippling grass. It had made him feel better.

"They're okay," he answered noncommittally, without much enthusiasm.

His grandfather looked at him for a moment. "Is there something on your mind, Matt?" he asked.

Matt looked thoughtful for a moment. "Yes. You know I plan on coming back here soon."

His grandfather didn't say anything.

"Well, I was thinking," Matt went on. "If I'm going to live here on the reserve, I want to learn more about my people. I was hoping you would tell me something about our family, and maybe stuff about the Tsuu T'ina, like stories the elders tell." His voice was starting to get excited. "And I've always wanted to have hair long enough I could wear in braids like the old days. I've started to grow it out already." He held up the very small ponytail he wore as proof of what he said.

"It's good to know where your roots are from. I can help you with that," his grandfather said, adjusting the snaffle on the bridle he'd brought with him. "But tell me, why this sudden interest in your family history? You were never one for the old stories when you lived here."

Matt suddenly looked uncomfortable. "No reason. It's just, you know, with the new family, Mom won't have much time to tell me the stories herself."

His grandfather nodded. He smiled like he knew something Matt didn't, then changed the subject.

"How about your sports? You playing for a new team now?" the old man asked as they moved farther into the recesses of the barn.

"I'm not playing basketball anymore," Matt said, trying to sound casual. "If I can't play for the Warriors, I don't want to play." He kicked at a stone on the floor.

His grandfather looked at him thoughtfully, then moved beside a stall that had been recently cleaned and was in need of fresh straw. He hung up the bridle.

"You know, Matt, over your lifetime, you will ride many ponies. Some of them will be really good horses, well broken with a brain in their heads who want nothing better than to please you; others will be sorry nags who will fight every inch of the way until you figure out how to make them do what you want. You can't always choose the easiest pony to ride. But you know something, Matt. Every one of those horses will teach you something valuable. All you have to do is hold onto the reins and listen to what the pony is trying to tell you." He chuckled to himself and headed toward the hayloft.

Matt knew what his grandfather was trying to say, but perhaps he didn't understand what Matt was feeling.

His grandfather pointed to some straw bales up in the loft and told Matt to lower down six for the horse stalls.

When Matt was younger, he and his grandfather had devised this tricky pulley system for lowering the heavy green bales down to the floor of the barn. Matt thought it was great, as it allowed him to ride the pulley rope up to the loft. He'd place the bale, with the rope attached, on the edge of the loft, then go down and put his foot in an old stirrup that was fixed to the other end of the rope. When Matt pulled, the bale would slide off the edge of the loft and up he'd go as the bale came down. It was a lot of fun.

When he was a kid, he'd gone up a lot faster. This summer, he and his grandfather planned on modifying the pulley so that two bales would come down at once. The speed with which he'd be rocketed up to the loft should increase dramatically — he still wasn't *that* big.

After they'd lowered all the bales, Matt dragged one over to the freshly cleaned horse stall and broke it open. He spread the sweet-smelling straw on the floor, ready for his grandfather's old horse, who was out in the pasture.

As they walked back to the house, Matt thought about what his grandfather had told him about the many ponies he would ride in his lifetime.

"I'm just going to wash up, Grandpa. I'll be there in a minute," he said as they entered the back porch on their way in for fresh lemonade. Matt turned the water on in the porch sink. Grandma always liked them to wash up before coming into her spotlessly clean house.

Matt had just finished wiping his hands off on a towel when Violet and Rosemary came bursting through the back door.

"Matty, you have to come with us. Daisy and Marigold are in trouble. Hurry!" they yelled and started pulling on his arm.

"Okay, okay, where are they?" he asked as he was jostled down the back steps.

"They're in the corral with one of the big horses. All they wanted to do was feed him some hay, then when they had no more left, the mean old horse wouldn't let them leave. They're stuck in the pen with him."

Matt walked around the corner of the barn and stared into the corral.

There were Marigold and Daisy, standing absolutely still while across from them, his grandfather's cantankerous old stallion, Tornado, was watching them with an evil glint in his eye.

"Oh no," Matt whispered under his breath. He'd sparred with the old stallion for years and knew how mean he could be. Up until now, the animal had never beaten Matt.

He slowly climbed up on the corral fence, keeping his eyes on the big horse. Tornado snorted suspiciously, sending a little dust devil whirling through the dirt.

"Hello, you miserable old pile of bones. Are you scaring those little girls?" he asked in a low, calm voice. "That's not very neighbourly of you." The stallion pawed the ground with one huge hoof.

"Marigold, Daisy, I want you to listen to me very carefully. When I tell you, I want you to run to that low spot over there and scoot under the fence as fast as you can." He pointed to an area in the corral where the ground had sunk and the space between the bottom rail on the fence and the ground was easily big enough for the two girls to scamper under.

He swung one leg over the top rail of the fence. Carefully, he lowered himself down into the corral.

He slowly walked over to stand between the two little girls and the old stallion, blocking them from the animal's view.

"Hey, you, remember me?" he asked, raising his arms to distract the horse.

The animal didn't move. He just swung his head from side to side as though trying to catch a glimpse of the girls, who were still standing rooted to the spot.

"This is going to take some persuading." He started to move to one side of the stallion, who was now trying to keep both Matt and the girls in his sight.

"Ready, girls?" he asked over his shoulder as he kept moving toward the side of the horse.

Suddenly, Matt ran up to Tornado and pushed the animal's huge rump for all he was worth, trying to get the animal to chase him.

"Run!" he yelled at the girls as he continued shoving on the horse, who couldn't seem to make up his mind which target to go for.

A hard slap on the back end convinced Tornado that Matt was his man. The angry animal snorted, whirling on Matt with surprising speed. With an earsplitting whinny, he charged after the scrambling boy.

"Yeeeehaaa!" Matt yelled as he sprinted for the side of the corral.

Tornado roared after him, sending a cloud of dust up into the sunny afternoon sky. Matt knew just the spot to head for. If he could make it to the watering trough, hop up and over it, then onto the fence, he'd be out of the old stallion's reach.

Matt had used this same watering trough tactic many times before and the animal never seemed to catch on. If Matt's luck held, today wouldn't be the day Tornado figured it out.

With a triumphant yell and a spectacular leap, Matt cleared the watering trough and scaled the fence before the angry animal realized he'd been tricked again. This was one place where his spring-loaded legs came in very handy.

Matt scrambled over the top rail of the fence just as Tornado snorted to a stop at the watering trough, stamping and pawing the ground in frustration.

"Yaah!" came the cheer from the other side of the corral, where Marigold, Daisy, Violet and Rosemary had all clambered up the fence and were leaning over, watching their new brother do his rodeo clown act.

Matt jumped down.

"Get down from there, all of you," he ordered. "Don't you know better than to climb into a fenced area with an animal you don't know? You could have been trampled." He glared at all four girls, who were looking very sorry — even Violet and

Rosemary. Matt suspected it was the older twins who'd encouraged the younger girls to climb into the corral.

"I don't want to spend my life baby-sitting a bunch of brats. Now get out of here, go on, get into the house," he said pointing, his tone dismissive.

Marigold and Daisy began to cry. All four little girls then turned and ran into the house yelling for their new and, hopefully, sympathetic mother.

Matt wasn't sure why he was acting this way. Was it anger because the girls had done something so obviously dumb or was he really just feeling relief that they were unharmed? Was that what was making his palms wet with sweat and that peculiar, weak feeling in his stomach? He took a deep, calming breath.

He'd never been beaten by old Tornado, but he'd grown up with the stallion and knew him well. Those two little girls had no idea how ornery that old animal could get and how close they'd come to getting hurt.

Later, Matt's mom came out onto the back porch, where Matt was enjoying his long-overdue glass of lemonade.

"You did a good thing, Matt." She smiled at her son.

Matt finished his drink and set the glass down on an old wooden box that served as a makeshift table. A drop of condensation ran down the outside of the glass and was instantly soaked up by the dry wood of the weathered old box.

He suddenly felt angry at everything. It was really crummy he had to leave the reserve and the Warriors, and it was unfair of his mom to expect him to turn into an instant older brother who always knew what to do and say.

"I don't like this new role I have of playing nursemaid to a bunch of gabbling geese." He looked at his mom. "I have enough trouble looking after myself sometimes without having to worry about whether some silly little girl has gone and fallen down a well."

His mom came and sat beside him. "I know this is a big adjustment for you, Matt. You've had a lot of changes to deal with and I'm proud of the way you're handling everything." She took his hand. "This is our life now and I hope you can come to accept it as easily as those little girls have. Do you know what they said when they came into the house?" She smiled warmly at Matt, who was looking out over the gently waving prairie grass as though he expected to see a coyote poke its head up and start to run.

"They said you'd rescued them from the wild horse in the pen and you were a real, live 'superhero.' The bravest, best brother anyone ever had and they can hardly wait to tell all their friends about how you saved them 'from being squashed like bugs.'"

Matt looked at her as she continued. "They also said you can climb fences faster than anybody they know." She ruffled his hair. "And now, Superhero, I think we'd better head for home. We're going to have a barbecue for supper and I've got some things to prepare."

Matt smiled sheepishly. He'd never been called a super-hero before.

His mom got up and walked to the door. "And speaking of horses, there's something you should think about," she said, pausing before she went inside. "Do you remember when you were six and you disobeyed me and went into the barn to see the new horse your grandfather had bought? You'd been told to stay away from that stallion, but you didn't listen. Do you remember what happened?"

She disappeared into the house to get the girls ready to leave.

Matt remembered the incident his mom was talking about. It had been the closest he'd ever come to being seriously hurt. In fact, he might have been killed if it weren't for his grandfather jumping into the stall and pulling the frenzied horse away. Matt had been huddled in the corner, trying to dodge the big horse's flailing hooves.

His grandfather's arm had been broken when the angry animal had kicked him as he tried to get at Matt.

Matt remembered his grandfather hadn't yelled at him or disciplined him in any way. He didn't have to. Every time Matt looked at his grandfather's arm in that cast, he'd felt terrible. He still felt bad when he thought about it. He'd never disobeyed his elders again. It had been an important lesson.

5

A Coach's Job Is Never Easy

Point Guard: And since the weekend, the Geese have been sweet as pie. Honestly, it's like some mother ship swooped in and replaced my rotten little stepsisters with these really nice kids!

Free Throw: It sounds like things might get liveable around your house.

Point Guard: At least until the next explosion! I just hope my superhero costume's not in the cleaners when it happens!!!

Free Throw: Hey, man, what your grandfather said makes sense. We can't control or pick a lot of the changes in our lives. We just have to make the best of them and move on. Like staying focused on the game. What if you just check out the Bandits? You never know, you might learn something new you can use when you go back to the Warriors. Just keep in mind, when we're in the big league, we're going to get traded lots of times and every team is going to expect 110 percent from us.

Point Guard: Look, I have my reasons for not joining the Bandits, okay!!!!

Matt knew he was coming down pretty hard on Free Throw. He tried to change the subject.

Let's drop it for now. We have more important stuff to discuss — like Alonzo Mourning and the Heat. Do you think he'll ever be able to control his temper???

Matt had needed to change the subject. As far as he was concerned, the Bandits were out and so was making any friends at this new school. He didn't need Bragg Creek School or their basketball team.

Matt and Free Throw spent the better part of an hour discussing what they considered acceptable behaviour on a basketball court.

They both decided that when they were in the NBA, they wouldn't resort to the hotdog tactics that some of the high-priced players used.

As Matt walked home, he thought about what his grandfather and Free Throw had said. Some of it, he had to admit, made sense.

* * *

Tuesday, Violet and Rosemary had to stay for band practice, which meant that Matt had to stay to walk home with the twins. He'd been in the library, but Free Throw wasn't on the Net so Matt had time to kill waiting for the girls.

Because the championship was closing in, the Bandits were having more practices than before. As he walked out of the library, Matt could hear them playing in the gym.

He tried to ignore the sounds he heard as he walked past the gym doors, but the shrill of the whistle, the squeak of soles on the floor and the rhythm of the ball as it was dribbled down the court were irresistible.

He still didn't want anything to do with the Bandits and he wouldn't betray the Warriors for anything, but would it hurt if he just watched for a while? Like Free Throw said, maybe he'd pick something up he could take back with him.

He decided he should eyeball the Bandits so he could check out their new plays. Matt reached for the door handle.

He made his way to the stands and found a seat in the corner. There was a break in the action as the team gathered around the coach to listen to him explain a new play.

As Matt waited for the team to start playing again, he thought back to last year. It still made him feel angry. The Warriors had been in a good position to clinch a playoff spot, then they'd played the Bragg Creek Bandits and Matt had run into John Beal. This guy had made it his personal mission to grind Matt into the hardwood every chance he got. He'd give Matt a particularly vicious block, then, as Matt went down, he'd make some comment about the Warriors sticking with their own kind. Matt had tried to stay out of the guy's way, but when you play man-to-man defence, and Beal was your man, it was impossible.

Matt wasn't the only one Beal nailed either. He was personally responsible for two other top-scoring Warriors being injured badly enough that they had to leave the game. Why he hadn't been thrown out of the game was still a mystery to Matt. He was a first-class goon, but he always made it look good for the ref. He was rarely given a foul for his hatchet-man style of play. Matt had thought about complaining to the officials, but since the Warriors had lost the game and with it a shot at the championship, he'd only look like a whining loser.

Suddenly the team meeting broke up and the Bandits hit the floor. The moment the team began moving the ball around, anyone watching could see they were good. They worked well together and each player knew the other's strengths and weaknesses. It was obvious these guys were very serious about the game. Matt grudgingly admitted to himself that this was something you had to respect in any team, even the Bandits.

Matt looked from player to player, searching for Beal. He couldn't see him with the players on the court and since Beal was so big, mean and ugly, he was pretty hard to miss. Glancing over at the players still on the bench, Matt was surprised to find the goon wasn't anywhere to be seen. Either he was away today, or he was no longer playing for the team. Not having to watch that guy play was fine with Matt, whatever the reason.

Matt settled back to watch the Bandits as they practised. One drill was particularly interesting to watch because it used a number of skills and required timing, speed and accuracy.

One player was placed as a pick near the basket at the far end of the court. Another player chose any of five types of passes to get the ball to his teammate, who would then dribble down court, dodge around the screen and go in for a lay-up. Their passes were crisp and on the mark, their dribbling smooth and controlled and their shooting ranked up with the best. Matt had to admit they were good.

Still, he thought resolutely, they were no Tsuu T'ina Warriors.

* * *

The next afternoon, Jazz and her team had a game after school. Matt and all the Geese stayed to watch.

The younger girls had brought noisemakers, which they blew every two seconds. Matt told them they should only use their horns when Jazz's team scored.

"But then we'll never get to blow them," Daisy complained, pouting and pushing her bottom lip out dramatically.

Matt couldn't argue. Jazz's team wasn't doing too well in the points department.

Matt watched them with a practised eye. He could see their weaknesses and knew he could help. If only Jazz would take him up on his offer and try some of the drills he'd suggested.

He watched his stepsister repeatedly consult her play-book, discuss her pick with coach Blande, the phys-ed teacher who doubled as a basketball coach, then put the play in motion only to end up trying a different strategy when the first one failed. Her ideas were good; the girls just didn't have the basic skills to make them work.

He could see how much she loved basketball and how much her team deserved to win. She worked hard with them, but it wasn't enough. To win, everyone on the team had to play their position like they owned it; one player couldn't cover for everyone else.

Watching Jazz play her heart out, Matt had to admit his stepsister was okay — on the court.

Jazz was centre for her team. Tall and agile, she easily won the tip-off, nudging the ball to the point guard, a short girl with curly brown hair and really quick hands.

Matt had watched this girl during the drills. She obviously felt her lack of height was something she couldn't overcome. For Matt, his height, or lack of it, had never been a drawback. He'd always been able to use it to his advantage. He was sure this girl could too, but she had to have the right mindset going in. Now, even when she had time to prepare, she would barely try to jump.

Then Matt noticed something odd. When she was caught off guard covering her opponent, the little point guard could jump with the best of them. If she wouldn't worry about having to jump and just do it instead, Matt was sure she'd be awesome.

The power forward continually telegraphed where she was going to pass the ball, making it easy to pick off her passes. That could be easily corrected, he thought to himself.

The small forward would fire her shots from well outside, but would have one air ball after another because she didn't have the accuracy for the distance she was shooting from. And whenever she had the ball and an offensive player started toward her, she passed it, even when the receiver was not in a good position. She was afraid of getting hit. He could see it.

As the game progressed, Matt made a mental note of everything he thought needed attention. Jazz had great hustle and was good in the paint, but she couldn't do everything. Her team needed to work together as a unit. When the final buzzer sounded, Matt felt bad for his stepsister. It was a humiliating loss.

The final score was 54-20, for the bad guys, as Rosemary said.

Matt's mom, who had to miss the game because of work, was waiting to pick everyone up.

Jazz threw her gym bag into the back of the van, then shook her head. "I think I'll walk. I'll see you at home." She turned and slowly started across the playground.

Matt hesitated, watching Jazz as she walked away. "You know, Mom, it's such a nice day, I think I'll walk home too." He closed the door and waved goodbye to the Geese, who were already in their seat belts.

His mom waved, then pulled out of the parking lot.

Matt ran to catch up with his stepsister.

As soon as they'd crossed the playground and started into the forest, Precious materialized out of the trees and silently fell into step beside Jazz and Matt. The big dog was always with Jazz when they were away from the house and Matt knew she smuggled the beast into her room at night. He couldn't believe any of the Geese hadn't found out about the dog yet. They were the snoopiest kids on earth. The word privacy meant nothing to them.

"Your team played hard today," he said casually, trying to break the ice.

Jazz didn't reply.

"You had some really good moves," he added.

"We still lost," Jazz said, throwing the stick she was holding. Precious ignored the invitation to play fetch.

They walked along in silence for a while. Finally Matt spoke again.

"I was watching closely and I think I saw a couple of places where your girls are weak. I could help you come up with some drills, if you want."

Jazz whirled and faced him. "I thought I told you we don't need any help. We had a bad game, that's all. We just need ... " She stopped, searching for what she wanted to say, then finished angrily, "We just need more practice." Clenching her fists, she continued, "And as for drills, I think I know what my players need a little better than you."

She turned and began to run, picking her way through the forest, Precious loping along beside her.

Matt watched her go. He knew what she was feeling. When you love the game, every win and every loss were important. They said things about your team — and if you were captain of that team, they said something about you.

6

Surprise Player on the Court

The Geese had been bugging him for a week to teach them how to "talk Indian." They'd decided that being able to speak another language could come in handy if they ever wanted to talk secretly in front of their friends. Matt suggested they take up French like every other normal Canadian kid.

They said that was the whole problem. Too many of their friends could already *parler français*. They needed something different.

Matt thought about teaching them to swear in Indian. After all, they'd never know, then decided he'd stick to *bunny rabbit* and *puppy dog*. His mom would throw a fit if she caught him teaching her precious new daughters anything but polite conversation.

His mom had a lot to learn about her little darlings, Matt thought. Still, he had to admit the Geese could make him laugh. It was either that or run away from home just to escape the brats.

Saturday his mom and stepdad were going to take the twins to a local amusement park. Thankfully, he didn't have to go. Neither did Jazz. She was going to wash his mom's catering van. She'd volunteered. Matt thought that was pretty nice of her.

The sunny May day turned out to be a scorcher. Matt's job was to make sure the new sod they'd laid in the front yard didn't get burnt to a crisp. He could handle that. In addition to a new basketball magazine he'd been dying to read, he had a hand-held video game that Collin had lent him. He could do both as he watched the grass grow.

A couple of the guys from Tsuu T'ina had stopped over earlier and were really impressed by the garage hoop and great setup he had. Matt had caught up with the local news, which included the revelation that a new kid, Jonathan Buffalo Runner, had moved to the reserve and he could jump nearly as high as the Cloud Leaper. They'd all laughed about this. After a couple of games of pickup, his Warrior teammates had left to go back to the reserve.

Matt thought about this Buffalo Runner guy. He didn't know anything about him except that he used to live with his mom in the city, and now he was going to live with his dad on the reserve. A big change like that must be really confusing for the guy. It was a good thing he had basketball to help with the adjustment.

He was just finishing watering the new grass, when Jazz came over to him.

"I need the hose to wash Mom's van," she stated, holding out her hand for the hose Matt held.

He was tempted to give it to her — wet end first.

But instead, he shut the water off and handed her the hose. "Sure, I'm done for a while anyway." He grabbed his basketball mag and walked over to the hammock he'd slung between two big poplar trees. He smiled at Jazz as he settled himself in the brightly coloured hammock.

From the look on her face, he expected to get a shower himself any minute.

He'd just started to read an article on Michael Jordan's contribution to the game, when he glanced over at Jazz.

She was busy scrubbing the van with an enthusiasm Matt found surprising. Precious, the big hairy beast, was lying on the concrete driveway in the shade of the garage, watching his new master as she worked.

Ordinarily, Matt would have just laid there and enjoyed watching someone else do a chore that he was supposed to be doing. But something about the way she was energetically getting out the polishing rags and wax made him feel a twinge of guilt.

Sighing, he walked over to her. "I would suggest ..." he began, then saw the warning look in her eyes when she looked up at him from her bag of wax rags. He held up his hands. "All I'm trying to do is make your job a little easier."

"Okay, Hot Shot, what?" she asked, tossing her long blonde braid over her shoulder.

"I'd suggest you wait until the van's in the shade from those trees before you wax." He motioned to the tall stand of pines that bordered the driveway. "The metal's got to be really hot and the wax will be hard to work with."

She hesitated for a minute, then nodded. "Okay, I didn't know that. Thanks for the tip." She looked at the sun, then at the trees. "I'd say we have about an hour." She glanced over at the basketball lying by the garage door. "Want to shoot a few hoops while we wait?"

Matt thought about this for a minute, but couldn't see any obvious traps or reasons why he shouldn't.

"Sure, you're on," he said, smiling at his stepsister.

Matt knew he would have to really try against Jazz. Jazz played as good as a guy. He made sure he kept the ball in close when he manoeuvred past his stepsister. She had wicked hands and could fake you out and take possession of the ball before you knew what had happened. Combine that with her killer lay-up and you had a player who was hard to beat.

The lead switched several times and Matt flat out hustled just to stay two points ahead of his stepsister.

Jazz soon learned about his awesome accuracy when it came to awkward shots. She also had a first-hand demonstration of the *Cloud Leaper* jump shot. Jazz was tall for a girl, but Matt had legs that could out-jump a guy a foot taller than he was. He almost felt guilty as he soared up and sent a perfect shot sailing through the net. Almost.

Another thing he found himself admiring about his stepsister was her persistence. She just never quit. Of course, Matt would never tell her that.

The afternoon sun had begun slipping down toward Moose Mountain in the west before they both agreed to call it quits.

Matt had to admit it had been an enjoyable afternoon. They'd managed to get along surprisingly well. Jazz could really play.

"We'd better get that van polished before everyone comes home," she said, wiping the sweat from her forehead and tossing Matt a can of Superbrite Car Polish.

"Hey, what's this *we* stuff?" he asked, trying to catch his breath. "As I recall, the deal was *you* do my chores, not a group effort." He held the can of polish out to her like it contained some toxic substance.

"And when I asked if *we* should have a game while *we* waited to polish the car, you agreed. Are you going back on your agreement?" she asked, that now-familiar edge back in her voice.

Matt shrugged, giving in. "I guess you got me on this one. Just remind me next time you invite me to join you in a friendly game, to have my lawyer read the fine print for tiger traps first."

He motioned toward the freshly sodded lawn. "First, I have to put the sprinkler on the grass by the side of the house."

They spent the next hour polishing the van until it gleamed. It looked great by the time they finally tossed their polishing cloths in the plastic bag Jazz had brought.

"Hey, not bad," Matt said, standing beside his stepsister as they admired their handiwork.

It was at this moment that Matt's gaze went beyond the van and over to the sprinkler watering the new grass.

"Oh no!" he groaned and started running. Jazz watched him for a second, confused, then saw the reason for Matt's panic.

Precious was busy digging huge holes in the soggy wet turf, then tossing the clumps up in the air before dislodging a new piece. The freshly sodded lawn was a black muddy quagmire of used-to-be grass.

"Precious! What have you done?" Jazz yelled at the now black dog. Precious, standing over the sprinkler with a piece of sod hanging out of his mouth, looked up in surprise.

Jazz continued running toward the mud-soaked dog.

"Jazz, don't run, he'll think you want to play chase ..." But before Matt could stop her, the dog had taken his cue from Jazz and began galumphing around the yard, swinging the soggy clod of grass.

Too late, Matt spied the open family room patio door. Precious sprinted across the muddy field and directly into the house — with the grassy prize still clamped firmly between his jaws.

Jazz and Matt looked at each other. "This is not good," Matt said and started after the big dog.

The house had been turned into an instant shambles. Precious had jumped on the family room couch, then leapt over the high-cushioned back and continued his tour of the house,

knocking bits of mud off the earth clod he carried as he
bumped into unfamiliar chairs and tables.

Jazz and Matt finally cornered the muddy monster lying
across Jazz's bed, wagging his tail triumphantly at being the
first to find a soft, dry place to end the game.

"Precious, how could you? You know you're not allowed
on the bed with muddy paws!" Jazz admonished.

It was then she noticed the dirty dog had dropped his
chunk of turf somewhere on his mad romp through the house
and now had Jazz's old *Fuzzy Bunny*, a favourite childhood
stuffed animal, clenched firmly in his huge jaws.

"Oh, no!" she wailed. "You can't have *Fuzzy Bunny!*" she
reached over and grabbed part of the toy that was sticking out
of the side of the dog's mouth. "Drop it!" she said firmly. The
dog didn't respond, except to clamp down a little harder on
the old toy.

Jazz became frantic. "I said *drop it*, you big, stinky —"
She began pulling on the toy, trying to dislodge it from the
dog's firmly closed mouth. Pulling with all her might, she
suddenly froze as she heard a terrible ripping sound.

She stood absolutely still, staring down at her hand, which
held the shredded pink leg of the old stuffed toy. "No, no, no!"
she shrieked.

Precious, terrified by Jazz's yelling, fled from the room,
the mutilated toy bunny still gripped in his jaws.

Matt was confused. "Jazz, what's the big deal. It's just an
old toy."

Jazz looked heartbroken. "You don't understand. My
mother gave me that bunny when I was just a little girl. It's
one of the few things I remember about her." She hugged the
muddy leg to her. "And now it's gone!" Jazz looked like she
might start crying.

Crying was not something Matt had much experience
with. He didn't know what to do. "Jazz, don't start crying.

We'll just go get the rest of the toy from Precious and you can sew the leg back on. A few weeks' rest and the rabbit will be good as new." He hoped his attempt at humour would cheer his stepsister. It didn't.

Jazz sniffed loudly. She reached for a tissue and blew her nose, and then she looked around. "Just look at this mess. When Mom and Dad come home, they're going to find out about Precious anyway. Everything's ruined."

Matt feared this was going to start a new round of sniffles, so he spoke up quickly. "Wait here while I go get the bunny, then we'll decide what to do about the mess." He left to find the dog.

He had no luck finding him as he searched the house. Next he tried the garage, then the shed where he slept. The dog was no where to be found and neither was the stuffed bunny.

Matt hurried back into the house. Jazz had taken the dirty bedspread off her bed and had put it in the washing machine.

"I think he's run off," he said. "But I'm sure he'll be back later."

"But what about *Fuzzy Bunny*? He'll be gone, lying in some ditch somewhere for the coyotes to eat."

Matt looked at her, puzzled. "Jazz, it's just a stuffed toy."

She shot him a warning look. "Not to me, it isn't."

Matt exhaled loudly. "Okay, here's the deal. You clean up the mess before Mom and your Dad get home. And" — he couldn't believe he was going to say this — "I'll go track down Precious and Fuzzy Bunny. They couldn't have gone too far."

Jazz looked at him, beaming. "Really? You'd do that for me?"

"Hey, I'm not all bad," he said. "Besides," he said, looking around the mud-spattered house, "I think I'm getting the better part of the bargain."

He grabbed his mom's birdwatching binoculars as he headed out the back door in search of the missing dog. Matt just hoped the bunny was still with the mutt when he found him.

* * *

The pale yellow moon was just starting to rise as Matt, exhausted after hours of chasing the elusive dog, started up the path that led to his house. At his side was the truant mutt. Matt wished for the twentieth time that he'd thought to take a leash when he'd set out to find the dog. He'd braided some thin willows into a makeshift collar and was holding firmly to it as the two of them approached the construction shed at the back of the house.

Matt was trying not to hurry the dog, as he was limping badly from a fall he had had when he had tried unsuccessfully to jump over a cattle guard. The dog had fallen hard, twisting one leg as he slipped through the metal rails on the cattle guard.

Matt wasn't feeling too great himself. His sleeve was torn where he'd snagged it on some barbed wire and one knee was gashed from when he'd tripped over a piece of deadfall and landed on a jagged rock. However, he smiled to himself as he patted the bulge in his T-shirt — *Fuzzy Bunny* was home!

Being careful not to make any noise or turn on the motion detector light, Matt led the tired dog into the shed and made him lie down on the old blankets that served as his bed.

Matt started checking the dog's leg. He was certain it was only a sprain, but wanted to make sure before he left the dog for the night.

Satisfied the dog was all right, Matt was just straightening up when the shed was suddenly filled with light.

7

New Player on the Home Team

Matt whirled and blinked, the sudden brightness tempo-rarily blinding him. Precious began growling low in his throat.

"It's me, Precious," Jazz said, pushing open the door and walking out of the shadows and into the light.

The relief Matt felt at seeing his stepsister framed in the doorway was quickly replaced with confusion as he stared past her into the darkness.

She hadn't come alone.

Within seconds, the tiny shed was filled as the rest of the family crowded in to see the dog.

"Oh, look at the poor puppy!" Violet said sympathetically.

"He needs a bubble bath!" Marigold observed, pressing her favourite old baby blanket to her nose.

"Is he our dirty doggy, Daddy?" Rosemary asked, and then started giggling at the way that particular string of words sounded.

Precious quickly figured out what to do with all the atten-tion. He lay his head down on the ground and began whimper-ing pitifully.

"Is he hurt?" Matt's mom asked him, pushing forward and approaching the dog.

"I think he just twisted his leg," Matt said, running a tired hand through his dishevelled hair.

"Colleen, maybe we should call the vet?" Matt's stepdad suggested, watching the dog, who was still whining.

"I think that might be a good idea," Matt's mom said, assessing the situation. "From the looks of the leg, Matt's right, it's a sprain, but it wouldn't hurt to get it checked." Her husband nodded and slipped out of the shed to go phone the vet.

Everyone crowded around the sad-looking dog, patting and fussing over him as they waited for the vet to arrive.

While the rest of the family was busy with Precious, Matt called Jazz aside. "What happened? Why did you tell them about the dog?" he asked, still confused.

"Because I felt guilty for not telling them about Precious in the first place. I don't like keeping secrets," she said defensively. "Besides," she said, grinning sheepishly at Matt, "they caught me with the whole huge muddy mess, so I had to come clean." She winced at her own bad pun.

Matt sighed, then nodded. "You were right to tell them. I feel better knowing I don't have to keep any secrets either." He grinned at her. "I'm a terrible liar and if Mom had asked me about some big old dog hiding out in the shed, I'd have told her everything." He reached inside his shirt. "By the way, I believe this belongs to you." He handed his stepsister the worn and dirty toy rabbit.

Jazz's face lit up in a 1,000-watt smile. *"Fuzzy Bunny!* You're home!" She hugged the worn toy as if it were a lost child. "Thanks, Matt. You don't know how much this means to me." She smiled warmly at him and Matt suspected that from then on, things were going to be different between his stepsister and him.

"Excuse me, you two," Matt's mom said, interrupting them in that calm voice that meant she had something serious to talk about. "Jazz, we have to talk about this dog. You realize you can't keep him if he belongs to someone else." She had a way of cutting to the bottom line that was impossible to ignore.

Jazz nodded her head. "I know, Mom. But when I found him, he had no collar or identification or anything. He was almost starved to death. I couldn't just abandon him. He needed help — he needed me."

Jazz's dad had joined them and now both parents looked at each other in that way parents do when they are communicating telepathically.

Matt saw his mother nod her head slightly at her husband.

"Okay, here's the deal," his stepdad began. "Jazz, you have to put up posters looking for the owner and ask around at local stores and the school. If no one calls to claim him, then we'll keep him — under one condition."

Here, Matt's mom took over. "You must look after the dog — that means feeding him and giving him fresh water, cleaning up after him and grooming him regularly *without being told*. If you make the decision you're old enough to have a dog, it's up to you to follow through without our checking up. Agreed?"

"Sure," said Jazz, while Matt nodded his assent.

"Yeah!" cried the Geese, who'd been eavesdropping, then started clapping and jumping up and down.

Jazz grinned, relief washing over her face. "This is great! I've never had a pet before. And Precious is really smart. He knows all sorts of things already, like he's not to get up on the bed with muddy paws or ..." she realized what she'd said and moved quickly to correct herself. "I mean I *could* train him not to get up on the bed with muddy paws if we let him sleep in my room at night." She was obviously a very happy twelve-year-old.

Matt's mom looked at him, a twinkle in her dark brown eyes. "And as for you, mister — I'm not convinced you weren't in on this from the beginning."

Matt shook his head. "Nope, not me. I'm just an innocent bystander." He grinned at his mom, who shook her head knowingly.

Just then, Dr. Samson, the mobile vet, pulled into the driveway. The next half-hour was spent poking and prodding the big dog, who seemed to enjoy all the special attention.

The vet assured Jazz that Precious just had a deep tissue injury and crate rest, along with some medication to treat the inflammation, was all that was needed for a full recovery. She also told the family she knew of no lost Great Pyrenees, which is the breed Precious turned out to be, but would let them know if she heard of anyone missing their dog.

After the evening's excitement, Matt was ready for bed. He figured he'd chased that crazy dog more than 15 kilometres through the worst bush around and his body felt every metre of the long hike.

Precious had been moved into the house, where his progress could be monitored more closely. The dog had not objected as he was tenderly escorted in and set up with a soft quilt and pillow to lie on.

Matt had found out that he, Jazz and his stepdad were going to spend all the next day repairing the damage Precious had done to what had been the newly sodded lawn.

As he lay there, trying to go to sleep, Matt could hear the Geese arguing over where Precious would sleep when he was well enough to climb the stairs. Jazz's voice cut through all the squawking, silencing the younger girls. Matt figured Jazz had laid down the law on whose dog it was and where *her* dog would sleep.

He smiled to himself, glad he was two floors down.

* * *

Point Guard: So now we have this big hairy dog that thinks he's a person. He's made himself right at home, like he's lived here his whole life. Jazz is really happy.

Free Throw: Speaking of your jockette sister, how's her team doing? Still problems with basic plays?

Point Guard: Yeah, which I wouldn't care about except she's not so bad, you know. She's really been treating me differently since the dismembered bunny episode. For a girl, she's okay.

Free Throw: So maybe now she'll let you give her some tips.

Point Guard: I'd be pushing our new ceasefire if I brought up b-ball. It's still a touchy subject.

Free Throw: But it's the GAME. It's every basketball player's sworn duty to try and play the best game he or she can and to do whatever they can to help his or her team WIN.

Point Guard: I agree, but she's a girl and STUBBORN. You know, Free Throw, it's a real shame to see her finessing the ball at the top of the key, then having a teammate toss a brick and ruin the play. Like it or not, I'm connected to Jazz and the idea of her playing on a losing team, well, you know, it might possibly, in a real stretch, reflect on my own greatness. (Ha! Ha!)

Free Throw: And she still won't take any advice directly from you?

Point Guard: I'm not even going to offer. She makes it way too difficult.

Free Throw: Too bad. I've got a couple of great plays I'd love to pass along and it sounds like her team is worth the effort.

Point Guard: Wait a minute!!!! I'm having one of my brilliant ideas! (You'll get used to these as time goes by!)

*What if she got some help without knowing it came from us.
She's smart enough to recognize a talented play or drill when
she sees it.*

*Free Throw: But how will you get her the info without her
knowing it came from us?*

Matt grinned to himself as he typed his answer in. This
was so simple: it was genius. He didn't know why he hadn't
thought of it before.

*Point Guard: You're going to love this, old Buddy. Jazz
has a playbook where she keeps all her notes on the game —
including handouts from the coach. All I have to do is sneak
the plays in without her knowing and going ballistic. That
way, she can decide whether she wants to use them without
any pressure from knowing two of the best future players in
the league are behind the whole thing!!!!*

*Free Throw: You ARE a genius. If she wants to use them,
they're right in front of her, but you realize, if she doesn't use
them, you can't say anything!!!*

*Point Guard: No worries. Jazz is smart enough to recog-
nize PURE GOLD when she sees it.*

*Free Throw: All I have to say is — devilishly clever, Mr.
Bond.*

Matt felt great. He really did want to help Jazz and her
team. He loved the game too much not to help a fellow player,
especially if that fellow player was a stepsister who loved
basketball as much as he did.

Besides, there was that other little thing. It was something
Jazz had done during the dog ordeal that had given her two
points on Matt's scoreboard. Jazz had accepted all the blame
connected with the dog herself, and not mentioned his name
once to their parents to deflect some of the heat onto Matt. He
knew his mom suspected that he'd known about the dog, but
Jazz had never implicated Matt in any way. It may not have
been a big thing to anyone else, but it was to Matt.

He and Free Throw spent most of their free time that afternoon refining plays and drills that Matt could slip into Jazz's playbook. They selected two drills that her team needed the most. If these went off okay, the rest would follow. He was looking forward to seeing if she used them. The only problem left, was how to get them into her playbook without her realizing where they came from.

While watching practice the next day, Matt was still trying to figure out that one, tiny problem. He placed his hand on his backpack, which had the computer printouts of the two drills he and Free Throw had decided were good starts. He'd even highlighted sections with a fluorescent hot pink marker to draw them to Jazz's attention.

Coach Blande had called the girls together and was explaining a finer point of the chest pass, when Matt saw Jazz excuse herself. The coach was sending her to his office to get an elastic knee support for one of the players. As Matt watched, he knew he was about to get his chance.

The coach began distributing some handouts with diagrams on them. Matt took his own play sheets out of his pack and stuffed them into his shirt pocket. Then he climbed down from his seat and walked over to the coach.

"Hi, I'm Matt — Jazz's stepbrother. I can take those handouts for her if you like. I'll put them with her playbook so they don't get lost." He held out his hand to the coach.

"Sure, that would be great, Matt. Thanks." Coach Blande smiled and handed Matt the papers.

Matt turned and headed to the bench area where he'd seen Jazz's playbook. As he walked, he pulled the play sheets out of his shirt pocket and slipped them into the pile.

He really hadn't done anything wrong. He'd simply delivered the handouts — *all* the handouts. The rest was up to Jazz.

* * *

It wasn't until later that week that Matt had a chance to see if Jazz had done anything with the drills. He couldn't really ask her if she liked any one drill more than another and, by the way, weren't the ones with the crazy pink highlighting great!

Matt stood at the gym doors and watched as Jazz had her girls run through what she considered the most important drills. He couldn't help grinning broadly as he noted they were the two that he and Free Throw had devised. As he turned to go to the library, he could hear his stepsister emphasizing in a loud voice that they were going to work on these until they got them right.

Matt and Free Throw came up with a series of great plays that a team like Jazz's would be able to use effectively. They were tricky to catch, but simple to execute. Matt felt good about helping, even if it was Jazz, he smiled to himself, the dragon lady of the court. Maybe he'd tell her someday, when they'd been related a little longer. In the meantime, he'd secretly slip the new material into his stepsister's playbook, first chance he got.

* * *

Matt and Free Throw's plays were put to the test in a game a couple of weeks later. This time, both parents, plus Matt and all the Geese were there to watch and again there were complaints because the twins didn't expect to be able to use their noisemakers.

"Just give Jazz and her team a chance," Matt admonished the pouting girls. "They just may surprise you."

From the second Jazz's team took the opening tip-off, Matt knew he was looking at a new, improved team. They suddenly had confidence as they stripped the ball from the other team and drove past the set picks to score off a great lay-up.

Matt watched as Jazz used the play he and Free Throw had come up with, time and time again, varying it just enough so that the other team's defence never caught on.

By the third quarter, Matt had turned into the noisiest fan in the auditorium.

He'd noticed how the point guard was really trying to jump and managed to get the ball a surprising number of times. The power forward's telegraphing was way down and the small forward was shooting from well inside, which made her shots much more effective.

It was as if Jazz had just been waiting for a key to moti- vate her girls and, Matt grinned to himself, he knew who had supplied it. He was sure Coach Blande would have been able to help Jazz eventually but Matt had seen these problems before, and knew just how to fix them.

The game was a noisy success. The twins had never used their noisemakers so much before. They were delighted. So was Matt.

"Wait till Free Throw hears about this! It worked!" He laughed as they all clapped loudly.

Violet looked at him, puzzled.

Later, the family had gone out to supper to celebrate what amounted to the team's first victory of the season. Matt had known they were bad, he just hadn't known how bad.

Their friend Robin brought a free round of pop to cele- brate Jazz's victory.

"Matty was sure happy for you, Jazz," Violet said, grin- ning. "In fact, he said he was going to tell his computer friend *it worked.*"

Matt took a big bite of his chicken finger. Jazz looked at him, confused.

"What had worked, Hot Shot?" she asked suspiciously.

Matt swallowed. "Oh, you know. The usual — hard work, diligence and practice, et cetera, et cetera." He hoped this sounded plausible. Things were going so smoothly.

"Well, I'm *glad* to see you learned something from this," Jazz said, apparently happy with his explanation. She began pouring a lot of gravy over her fries. "I told you I knew what was best for my team. You can now get on with your own career in the NBA and leave mine alone!" She smiled smugly. "I knew just what my team needed to hone their skills to razor sharpness. You see, Hot Shot," she said, grinning at Matt, "we didn't need your unwanted help, did we? And," she continued, pausing dramatically, a French fry held aloft, "this is just the beginning!" A large gob of gravy dripped off the fry and landed with a plop on her new jeans. "Rats!" she mumbled, stuffing the fry in her mouth and reaching for a napkin.

"You know what I'm glad of," Daisy asked, smiling sweetly at Jazz.

"What, Daisy dear?" Jazz said, smiling back at her sister.

"I'm glad it wasn't me who dripped *yuck* on your new jeans!" She put her hand up to her mouth and started giggling uncontrollably.

Jazz tried to look indignant, then she started giggling too. After all, it *was* pretty funny.

8

Win Some, Lose Some

Matt had to admit that since Jazz's team had started winning, she was a lot easier to get along with. In fact, it had started to be a regular routine for Matt and Jazz to play a few games of HORSE after supper. HORSE was an old basketball game where the first player makes a shot, usually a really tricky one. The other players try one by one to make a basket using the same shot, but if one of them misses, this player earns a letter, and the next player in the line gets to make up a new shot. The players take turns trying to outshoot each other until someone has accumulated all the letters in the word HORSE. This guy's the big loser. Matt and Jazz always made sure they used the hardest shots possible in an effort to out shoot each other. Usually the game stayed pretty even, with each of them missing about the same number of shots and accumulating the same number of letters. There had been more than one night where the E had decided the loser.

One particularly warm evening, they were busy playing another round of HORSE, when Jazz's dad came out and leaned against the garage wall, watching them play.

"Hi, you two. Your mother's taken the girls for ice cream, and since it's such a beautiful night, I thought I'd just stay out here for a while. Hope you don't mind the peanut gallery." He smiled at Matt and Jazz as he retrieved a lawn chair from the garage and set himself up at the side of the driveway.

Jazz and Matt were tied with HO each, when the phone rang. Immediately, Jazz tossed the ball to Matt.

"I'll get that. I'm expecting a call." She dashed into the house before Matt could say anything. He could have sworn her face was a brighter shade of pink than it had been a second before.

"I think Jazz might have a secret admirer," his stepdad said, getting out of the lawn chair. "How about I fill in while she's tied up."

Matt felt sort of awkward. "Sure," he said casually. An odd thought flashed through his mind. What if he pushed his stepfather too hard and the old guy (he was two years older than his mom) had a heart attack or something? Matt didn't think chartered accountants did much roadwork to stay in shape. He decided to start off slowly so the exertion wouldn't shock his stepdad's system.

"Let's take turns shooting," he said, passing the ball as slowly as possible to his stepdad.

"Sounds good to me," his stepdad agreed. They spent several minutes just trying to put the ball in the basket, nothing fancy.

"You know, I'm really glad there's another man in the house," his stepdad began after an unsuccessful rattler. "You have no idea how the girls' constant conversation can drive a guy crazy. If it weren't for Jazz's interest in basketball, I'd never get to talk about anything but Barbie and Barney." He lobbed a high arcing effort that missed again.

Matt retrieved the ball. Had he heard right? The Geese even got on their own father's nerves! He did a great jump shot — swish. Nothing but net! Man, he loved that sound!

Before his stepdad could move, Matt ran up for the ball and passed it to him. No sense taking chances in this heat.

His stepdad went on. "You know, Matt, I really admire the way you've jumped in and helped out with the twins. I know they can be quite a handful and, from everything I've read, it's only going to get worse. But I figure if we guys stick together, we can make it through at least until they're old enough to leave home." He smiled at Matt and fired a perfect chest pass to him.

They played a while longer in silence. Matt was too astounded by this last comment to speak. He was starting to feel more normal by the minute.

Then his stepdad actually sunk a basket. "All right! I'm back!" he said, grinning at Matt, who nodded and went to grab the ball. "I suppose you like other sports besides basketball?" his stepdad asked as he tried another set shot. This one was an air ball that rebounded off the side of the garage with a loud thunk.

"Nice try," Matt said, snagging the ball as it bounced past. "Yeah, I guess. I like hockey and football, but you know, just to watch." He jumped and shot, easily sinking the ball.

"Hey, I played hockey when I was younger," his stepdad said. "It was my winter sport." He watched Matt retrieve the rebound.

"What did you play in the summer?" Matt asked, genuinely interested now.

"Rugby," his stepdad answered, sporting a mischievous grin. With a move that was blindingly quick, he snagged the ball from Matt, who was dribbling past, then streaked in for a perfect lay-up. "I think it's all coming back to me now." He winked at Matt. "Care for a little game?"

Matt, surprised at his stepdad's speed and agility, grinned and nodded. "You're on ..." He hesitated, fumbling for the correct way of addressing this man.

"*Gordon* would be okay with me, Matt." He smiled at his stepson and tossed him the ball.

Matt and his stepdad played until the yard light blinked on. The score was close and several times, Gordon was leading. Matt was really enjoying himself and he was getting a killer workout.

"Aren't you two ever coming in?" Matt's mom called from the kitchen window, which overlooked the backyard. It was only then that Matt realized how long they'd been playing. He had no idea what had happened to Jazz. Whoever it was on the phone, he or she must have had an awful lot to say.

Matt and his stepdad headed into the house. Jazz was still yakking away on the family room extension. Her voice sounded sort of odd to Matt, sappy almost, and giddy. Not like Jazz at all.

"I told you it was a secret admirer," his stepdad said out of the corner of his mouth, but loud enough that Jazz could hear.

"Oh, Daddy, cut it out!" Jazz protested, but Matt could see her blush clear across the family room.

"I think we earned us a couple of orange ice cream floats, don't you, Matt?" his stepdad asked as they headed up the small set of stairs by Matt's room.

"Sure ... *Gordon*," Matt agreed, following his stepdad and leaving Jazz to continue her two-hour conversation.

* * *

Free Throw: That is so cool ! You actually call your stepdad by his first name. It makes me wish I could play hoops with my dad, but that's out of the question. Did you find out whom your stepsister ditched you for?

Point Guard: You're never going to believe this — it's Cory Cook! He's captain of the Bandits. And from the mushy way she was talking, I don't think they were just talking about the latest NBA basketball scores. Speaking of basketball, wait till I tell you about this great play I thought we could give to Jazz ...

With that, Matt launched into a long, detailed description of his play and how and when Jazz could use it.

Free Throw agreed and even offered a slight modification that allowed more than one position to initiate the play. He began typing what Matt knew was going to be a long explanation for the play.

Matt slipped out of the library to get a drink and laughed when he came back and the computer screen showed Free Throw was still typing the very wordy message for the *slight* modification.

By the time Matt left the school library, he was feeling great. Everything was going so well. If he couldn't play the game, this was the next best thing. In fact, he felt a little like a secret coach.

Matt strolled into the gym and right away, he knew something was wrong.

The other members of Jazz's team had already left, but Jazz was talking very animatedly with the coach. Her ponytail was swinging vigorously from side to side as she waved her arms up and down. Matt saw she had some papers clutched in her hands. Even from across the gym, he could see they had fluorescent, hot pink highlighting on them.

The jig, as they say, was up!

9

Sixth Man

Just then Jazz spotted him standing at the doors. She finished talking to the coach, grabbed her gym bag and stormed across the floor toward Matt.

He decided to wait for her outside.

Jazz slammed out the school doors past Matt and headed across the field for home. Matt hurriedly caught up with her.

"How could you do it?" she asked through gritted teeth. "After I told you my team could win without your interfering. What gives you the right to just ignore me and go ahead and do whatever you want?"

Precious had been waiting outside the school for them and was now trotting at Jazz's side. Matt could see the dog was confused at Jazz's angry tone. He hadn't done anything bad, but here was his master yelling and waving her arms around.

Matt understood how the dog felt.

"I only did it because I wanted to help you and your team play the best game you were capable of," he said in what sounded like a pretty weak defence, even to him.

He knew he was a sucker for punishment, but he had to ask. "Jazz, how did you find out about the drills I added to your playbook?"

"I found out," she said as she started fumbling with her backpack, "about your stupid meddling." She dumped the entire contents of the pack on the ground. "I found out because of this!" She held up the fluorescent hot pink marker.

"Oh," Matt said by way of adding to his now pitifully weak defence.

"I needed another copy of this week's new drill due to an unfortunate accident involving Precious, so I went to Coach Blande. How foolish of me to assume the drill came from him!" She started stuffing all her assorted paraphernalia back into her pack. "He told me he hadn't handed out those sheets. Then when I asked if he had any idea how the plays got in my book, he told me the only time he'd seen anyone near my playbook was when my sweet stepbrother was kind enough to put away some handouts for me while I was off on some mission of mercy, well ..." She took a deep breath and stood up, dusting her jeans off. "It didn't take a rocket surgeon to figure out where the rest of the mystery plays came from." She slung her pack over her shoulder, narrowly missing Matt's head. "Especially after today when I checked your pack while you were out of the library for a minute and, surprise, what did I find?"

She threw the marker at Matt. "I couldn't believe you'd do such a low-down, underhanded thing, so I went back to the gym and showed the coach all the highlighted plays. He says he doesn't even own a pink highlighter, but could he have a copy of the plays to use in his coaching!"

Matt thought that was quite a compliment. He couldn't say so, of course, but he filed it away to tell Free Throw next time he was on the Net.

"Look, I really am sorry, not about giving you the drills and plays — your team needed them — but about the way I had to do it. I should have shown the plays to you first, then let you decide for yourself whether to use them or not. It's just," he said with a long sigh, "I know how much you love the game and I knew your team really deserved to win."

Jazz's face momentarily softened. "You know what your real problem is, Hot Shot? You miss the game so much it's driving you nuts." Then her lips returned to the hard line they'd been set in while listening to Matt's explanation. "If you ever do anything like that again, I'll, I'll ... " She foundered, looking for exactly the right thing to threaten him with. "I'll cut off one of your stupid braids!"

This shocked Matt. He instinctively reached up and covered one of the very short braids he'd started to wear.

With a toss of her own long blonde hair, Jazz turned away and started for home. Matt had never seen her like this. It made him feel terrible since her incredible anger was directed right at him and he feared he'd probably finished the new friendship that he and Jazz had been enjoying. A couple of weeks ago, that wouldn't have mattered to him, but lately, he'd really started to like his stepsister.

* * *

They didn't speak to one another for the rest of that day or all the next. Matt's mom had noticed his glum mood and he'd given her the shortened version of the problem.

After supper Matt had heard his mom talking to Jazz in the kitchen, but he'd gone downstairs to his room to avoid another confrontation.

At school, on the third day of the big feud, Matt and Jazz were still avoiding each other like the plague.

The silent treatment was really starting to get to Matt.

"This is ridiculous," he mumbled to himself as he headed for the gym after school. He knew Jazz was going to watch the Bandits practise and he was going to resolve this once and for all. She had to listen to reason.

When he walked in, he saw Jazz talking to Cory Cook. From the way they were both talking and smiling, it didn't look like her admirer was very secret. Matt waited for her to finish talking to Cory.

Just then, Jazz spotted him standing by the doors. She smiled at him and waved. Matt thought this was very scary behaviour considering the last couple of days. He hesitated a moment, then waved back. Both Jazz and Cory started over toward him.

Matt wondered if Jazz was going to have her new boyfriend beat him up. He pulled himself up to his full height, which, on Cory, was about the top of the tall centre's shoulder.

"Hello, Matt," Jazz said sweetly.

Matt nodded at his stepsister. "Ah, hi Jazz. What's going on?" he asked suspiciously. Things were really strange.

She continued in that weird voice that made Matt want to look for the concealed weapon.

"Why, Matt," she began in the syrupy sweet voice. "I was just thinking about how much you love the game and not being able to play, and well," she continued, grinning slyly at him, "after talking to Mom, I decided to have a chat with Cory and the coach. They've agreed to let you be the sixth man for today's practice." She held up her hand to stop his protest, should he try one. "Don't thank me, stepbrother."

Then, abruptly, her tone changed and her voice grew soft and serious. "Matt, anyone who loves basketball as much as you do should always be playing. At least give the Bandits a chance. Who knows, you may even like it." She smiled at him and Matt knew things were okay with her again. He'd have to thank his mom when he got home.

Her words finally sunk home. He was supposed to be sixth man for the Bandits. Impossible! "Jazz, I know you're trying to do a good thing for me, but I can't." This was hard. He had to find a way out of this without hurting Jazz's feelings. He tried to think up a quick excuse. "I don't have my stuff with me."

Grinning, she handed him the brown paper bag she'd been carrying. "Mom packed this for you."

Matt looked inside the bag. It had his gym clothes and his Nikes along with a bottle of Gatorade.

"Actually," Cory added, "Jazz didn't have to try too hard to talk me into asking you. We really could use another player, especially if you're as good as Jazz says you are. You'd be doing me a favour by filling in for one of our missing guys."

Matt looked Cory right in the eye. "This missing guy wouldn't be John Beal, would it?" he asked.

Cory looked a little embarrassed. "As a matter of fact, yes. Beal didn't really *fit in* with the Bandits' style of play."

When Cory looked at Matt, Matt understood what Cory was trying to say.

Matt felt good and bad at the same time.

Good, because he really did want to play again and without that goon Beal on the squad. That guy was bad news from beginning to end and Matt wouldn't have played on a team who supported his style of hack-and-slash play. And bad, because he felt he was somehow turning his back on the Warriors. They were still his team.

"Jazz, I appreciate what you've done, but you know I'm a Tsuu T'ina Warrior. It wouldn't be right for me to play with another team."

"You're not *playing*, Hot Shot, you're just the sixth man at a practice game. For all you know, you might be riding the pine for the whole show." Jazz flipped her ponytail over her shoulder. "And now, you should get changed, and I'm going to go get a good seat before they're all gone." She turned and headed for the bleachers, which, Matt noticed, were 99 percent empty.

"Don't worry, Matt. Your sister explained you're going back to your old school to play with the Warriors. No pressure, I promise." He nodded at Matt. "I'll leave it up to you." He turned and went back to the team.

Matt was torn. He didn't know what to do. Then he thought of how Jazz had set everything up. She was okay and he knew she was doing this because she understood how much he loved basketball.

He did have to keep his skills up or he'd be no good to the Warriors when he finally managed to get back and he would get to know all their plays for the next time they played against each other. He went to change.

* * *

The practice started off pretty bumpy. A lot of the other players who were new to the team and hadn't played against the Warriors yet, took one look at Matt's height, or lack of it, and wondered what kind of a charity case Cory had signed up. They also thought his braids were "really different," as one player put it.

Matt just took it all in stride. He'd heard it before. It wouldn't matter once he was on the court. It was then his height became an advantage.

"Matt, you're in for Johnson. You'll play point guard," the coach said.

Matt got up and went to the scorer's table. He waited till the whistle blew, then went to sub for Johnson. He noticed he was subbing for the first-string players and was flattered.

The second the ball was inbound, he could feel that old excitement starting. It felt good to be playing again.

He didn't feel like he was at a disadvantage, even though he was new, because he'd been watching these guys play and had even played against some of the older players. He knew a lot of their moves already. To many of the players, however, he was an unknown.

He intercepted a pass right away and started down court. He was fast and he knew it. Before the others could catch him, he was at the top of the key and driving in for a perfect lay-up.

Swish! The sound was magical in his ears. He heard Jazz cheering from the bleachers.

The next chance he got was due to a personal foul. Matt stepped up to the line and licked his dry lips. He had a nasty tendency to mess up on free throws, but this time he willed himself to relax and concentrate on his stance. When he was comfortable, he let the ball go, imagining he was putting his hand right into the basket. The ball made a perfect arc and swished through the net. Matt felt himself smiling. In fact, he felt great. It was as if he could do no wrong.

The rest of the players on the team were starting to sit up and take notice now. He knew they'd figure it out pretty quickly. He didn't mind.

The next scoring chance came when Matt was moving the ball into the forecourt. He saw the shooting guard, Larry Chang, moving into a perfect scoring position. The other squad was putting on a lot of defensive pressure, but Matt managed a great pump fake, throwing his man off, then rifled the ball to Larry, who went up in a really impressive jump shot and snapped the ball home.

When Matt found himself covered by Eric Sooter, a huge, hulking swingman, he managed a slick spin deke, ducking under the arm of the big Neanderthal and firing a bounce pass to Ron Klassen, a small forward, who powered his way up to the net and hammered the ball in.

The opposing squad was not doing too well, but rallied to sink three baskets in a row.

When Matt formed up in the circle for the tip-off, he knew every eye was on him. He waited, feeling his heart beating strongly in his chest. The ref blew the whistle and tossed the ball high in the air.

Matt gathered himself for the jump, then, taking a deep breath, launched. He felt like he was a bird. He went straight up ... and up! He was easily 6 inches above his opponent, the big swingman, whose large, hairy arm he'd ducked under when sending the bounce pass to Ron Klassen. The guy couldn't believe what he was seeing as Matt's smiling face went up past his shaggy head. He seemed stunned.

Matt tipped the ball to Larry Chang, the shooting guard, who jumped, grabbed and headed for the net. Matt came running down to help block for Larry, who had really superior speed if he could get a clear path through traffic. Matt made sure he had that path and Larry went all the way — two points, no sweat!

"Way to go, Cloud Leaper!" Jazz yelled from the stands.

Matt felt good. He gave Jazz the thumbs-up and hustled to take his place for the next play.

The rest of the practice had Matt in on most of the action. His passing was right on and he'd never been so great at driving in lay-ups. He was interacting really well with the team by the time practice was over. He could work the plays, partly because he'd been watching the Bandits for a while, but mostly because of that sixth sense he seemed to have when it came to sizing up the way a play was going down.

In the closing seconds of the practice, Cory passed him the ball. "How about a shot from downtown?" he called.

Matt was outside the three-point line, way outside. The three-point line was an arc, 22 feet away from the basket and, even in the NBA, a success rate of 33 percent was considered good. The chances of his scoring were slim to nil, but that didn't stop him from trying. He grinned at Cory, then pulled the ball into his hip and sent it arcing high and directly at the net. Wham! It hit the backboard and bounced back deep into the court.

The buzzer sounded, ending the practice game.

"Good try, Matt," Cory called.

All the guys crowded around, congratulating Matt on a great performance.

"You were unbelievable, Matt!" Cory said, slapping him on the back. "Man, when Jazz said you knew b-ball, she wasn't kidding!"

"Where did you learn to jump like that?" Ron Klassen, the small forward asked, wiping his neck with a towel. "I couldn't believe it. You took off like a Saturn booster rocket."

"I missed the last shot," Matt said modestly. He wasn't used to all the praise.

"Yeah, but you sunk the rest," Larry Chang laughed. "Not bad for your first time out with the Bandits."

"You were great, Cloud Leaper," Jazz said, walking up to the group and smiling at her stepbrother.

"*Cloud Leaper*," Cory said, smiling at Matt. "I can see why."

"Yeah, that's what my teammates on the Warriors call me, because I can jump pretty good."

"*Pretty good*, Matt, you're the man!" Cory gave him a friendly punch on the arm.

Talking about the Warriors made Matt remember why he was here. He was supposed to be honing his skills and picking up strategies from a rival team. He shouldn't be standing here being the centre of attention and, he thought guiltily, enjoying it.

"Look, Cory, thanks for letting me be your sixth man, but I've got to go." He walked over to the bench and grabbed his gear.

"Hey, wait a minute. What about the Bandits? Aren't you interested?" Jazz asked, confused.

Matt knew she'd arranged this playing time with the Bandits because she understood how much he missed the game and wanted to play again, but he couldn't do it.

"Jazz, playing for the Bandits is out of the question." He nodded at Cory. "Thanks, but I just can't."

He shot Jazz a quick glance, hoping she knew him well enough to understand what he was trying to tell her.

"Sure," Jazz said slowly, nodding at him. "See you at home."

Matt turned away and walked across the gym floor, pushing open the doors without looking back.

10

Changes in the Lineup

When Matt left the building, he found himself smack in the middle of a cold early-summer downpour. He thought about going back into the school to wait it out, but decided he'd rather walk home in the rain than chance talking to Jazz or any of the Bandits.

By the time he reached their house, he was soaked to the skin and thoroughly chilled. Rocky Mountain rain always stayed cold, even later in the year when the summer heat was at its warmest.

"Matt, why didn't you wait for the rain to stop?" his mom asked as soon as he walked into the kitchen. "Your lips are practically blue. Go change and I'll make you a hot chocolate."

Matt did as he was told. He felt too crummy to argue.

When he came back into the kitchen, his mom set a steaming mug of hot chocolate in front of him.

"Okay, what happened? You have more sense than to walk home during a monsoon."

Matt knew he'd better come clean because Jazz would be sure to blab the second she got home. Having a sister who was beginning to care about him had its drawbacks.

"It's just, well, Jazz set it up so I could have a basketball practice with the Bandits and it went really well." He took a sip of his chocolate, realizing that the sticky white foam on top was marshmallows, which he loved.

His mom looked at him with a puzzled smile. "Let me get this straight. Your sister, who cares about you a lot, arranged for you to play basketball, a game you love, and this game went so well you risked double pneumonia to get away? Yes, I can see that."

She gave him a questioning look. "You're still not thinking about going back to the reserve and the Warriors are you, Matt? I though that was all cleared up. You seemed to be settling into your new life really well."

"It's not that, Mom, it's okay here. I'm even used to the Geese. It's just I still feel like my real home is on the reserve. I still feel like a visitor here sometimes."

His mom put down the recipe card she'd been reading and pulled out a chair across from him. "When, Matt? When is it you feel like a visitor?" She looked into her son's face. "I'd really like to know," she said seriously.

He thought about this. "Well, I'm okay at home, even with the Geese asking all their dumb questions. I also don't mind Jazz and her hairy monster. And you and Gordon are okay. In fact, ever since that killer game of pickup we had, I've gotten along pretty well with Gordon." He gave his mom a small smile.

His mom patted his hand and smiled back. She'd noticed the change between her husband and son. "Okay, you're doing well. What's left?"

He thought a moment and went on. "School's all right. I'm getting used to my teachers and I even like some of my new classmates, like Collin, the guy from the library who showed me how to use the Internet."

He grinned. "The Net is a blast, Mom, and Free Throw's become my best friend." He nodded his head. "I've told him things I wouldn't dare tell anyone else. It's like we've known each other for years and know each other's deepest, darkest secrets."

Matt had Collin to thank for that. He'd talked to the cyber-freak a few times since then and Collin had always been really friendly and helpful. He even said hi to Matt when they passed in the hall or met in Bragg Creek.

That only left one area that could have caused him to feel like he was at odds with his world.

He sighed. "I guess the time I feel like I don't belong here," he said, staring at his empty cup, "is when I play basketball." He looked up at his mother's eyes, hoping she would understand. "I'm a Tsuu T'ina Warrior, Mom, and I'll never be anything else." He pushed the cup away.

"Is that really the way you feel, or is that the way you think you're *supposed* to feel?" She gave him a second for the full meaning of her words to sink in. "I know you believe you owe your old team something, Matt, but don't you think you *owe yourself* something first? And if your Warrior teammates are really your friends, they'll understand your moving on, they'd even be glad for you. It's part of life. There will always be new things, places and people, that's what makes life so interesting. The secret to really enjoying the whole thing is to not quit — not on your dreams and not on yourself."

Matt looked at her. He didn't know what to say.

"I think you should go over and visit your teammates at Tsuu T'ina School. Talk to them. You say they're your friends, well, find out just what kind of friends they are." She got up and went back to her recipe cards.

Matt didn't say anything; he just went down to his room to think.

He'd been lying on his bed, staring at the white stippled ceiling for about half an hour when he decided maybe his mom was right — he should go talk to his buddies. He got up and called Jimmy Big Bear. The next practice was Thursday, after school. He'd ask his mom if she could drive him over.

* * *

The second the final bell rang on Thursday afternoon, Matt raced to the parking lot and his mom's waiting van.

He tossed his bag, which also contained his gym clothes and shoes, into the back and climbed in. He was excited. He was going to meet the Warriors.

"Okay, let's go!" he grinned at his mom.

"Aren't you forgetting something? The Geese!" She rolled her eyes. "Good lord, now you've got me calling them *Geese*!"

In his excitement, he'd forgotten this was to be a family outing. Impatiently, he scanned the front doors for his stepsisters. After what seemed an eternity, all five of them came strolling out. Marigold and Daisy were gleefully waving their latest masterpieces, which were destined to be showcased on the door of the refrigerator. From what Matt could see, Picasso had nothing to worry about.

Violet and Rosemary had their arms full of mystery bags and containers which, combined with the cardboard box with holes in the lid that Jazz was carrying, made Matt feel a little apprehensive.

Matt's mom had brought Precious, who'd been sleeping peacefully in the back until he heard the twins yelling. Instantly, he was up and trying to get to the front of the van so he could go investigate.

"Stay back there, boy. I've got a feeling we'll find out soon enough what's going on." Matt waited as the girls piled into the van. The air was instantly filled with the aroma of cedar wood chips.

"What's in the box, girls?" their mother asked, as she tried to hide a grin.

Violet and Rosemary looked at one another. "Well, Mom," Rosemary began. "It's like this. Jazz gets to have Precious for her own dog, so we decided we wanted a pet of our very own too." They both beamed at their new mom like that explained everything.

"And so you ... what?" their mom prompted.

"So we volunteered a nice home for our class guinea pig ... s." Violet smiled sweetly.

"You mean you have a live guinea pig in that box?" Matt asked.

"Actually," Rosemary said slowly, "two, and of course they're *alive*. They're best friends and we couldn't take one and leave the other and two are just as easy to look after as one and Mrs. McCarthy gave us cedar shavings and food and a waterbottle and everything ..." Her voice trailed off as she ran out of breath and convincing arguments.

Violet jumped in where her sister had left off. "We meant to ask you, but we just were so excited we forgot. We'll look after Arthur and Guinevere, Mom, honest, cross our throats and hope to choke." She made an *X* on her neck, then grabbed it with both hands and squeezed, sticking her tongue out to emphasize just how real this pledge was. "We'll clean their cage every day, just as soon as we go to the store and buy one. Can we get one of those Habitat things, so they can run around through the tunnels? Wait till Grandpa and Grandma see them! They'll love them just like us!" Her sales pitch complete, she looked at her mom hopefully.

Both girls then fell silent, awaiting the verdict. They watched their mother expectantly.

Matt's mom looked from Rosemary to Violet, then began what he knew was going to be a *mom speech*. "I want you all to understand that it's important you check with your dad and me before you decide to bring home any new pets. Jazz, that especially goes for you." She looked at Jazz, who nodded, knowing she couldn't say anything. "However, your teacher was kind enough to call and warn me about the new additions in case you two *forgot* to clear it with me. We decided you can keep Arthur and Guinevere on one condition." She looked at Rosemary and Violet. "You have to write a report on how you look after your new pets and give it to Mrs. McCarthy in September."

Marigold and Daisy, who had been quietly listening up till now, clapped their hands.

"Yeah! We'll do it!" Rosemary said, while Violet nodded happily.

"Well, I guess that's settled. Now, put the box on the floor and buckle your seat belts. We'll go show your grandparents the new additions to the household."

"You know," Matt said quietly, "if I were you, I'd be really careful when you walk your new pets." He looked back at Rosemary and Violet, who were busy positioning the box carrying the guinea pigs on the floor exactly between the two of them.

"Why?" Rosemary asked, reaching into the box and placing both animals on the side of the box closest to her.

"You wouldn't want anything to happen to them, would you?" he asked.

"Like what?" Violet asked, moving the two rodents to the other side of the box, which put them closest to her.

"Oh, I was just thinking about how on the reserve, a cougar came out of the woods last year and grabbed a dog right off Mr. Spotted Elk's porch," Matt said casually.

Both girls stopped rearranging the guinea pigs and stared at him.

"And then there's the problem of hawks. They can carry off guinea pigs so fast, they'd just be a speck in the sky before you knew what happened." He could see Violet's lip beginning to quiver.

"Matthew Eagletail, you stop telling stories like that!" his mother said, scowling.

Matt knew he'd better lighten up a little or he'd have two bawling geese on his hands.

He grinned at the twins. "I was just kidding. As a matter of fact, everyone knows you're supposed to walk guinea pigs under an umbrella, that way no hawks will spot them and they'll be absolutely safe." This seemed to help a little.

"Anyway, you don't have to worry about your old *ninny pigs*," he added, buckling his own seat belt on. "What self-respecting hawk would want those scrawny little things when it could swoop down and scoop up a nice fat bunny!"

"Matthew!" his mother snapped. As Matt turned away from the girls, he noticed they were both sitting absolutely rigid in their seats, their mouths open and a shocked look on their faces.

However, by the time his mom dropped Matt off at Tsuu T'ina School, everyone was laughing as a detailed plan for looking after the two guinea pigs was worked out, complete with an exercise schedule that involved two small cat harnesses and leashes to safely walk the rodents.

Rosemary and Violet both insisted they also wanted umbrellas, even after Matt told them repeatedly he'd been kidding about needing the extra safety feature. Feeling a little guilty for scaring the small girls, Matt offered to find them each an umbrella and check the sky for hawks before each walk.

He waved goodbye to his new family and, as the van turned onto the main road, he wondered what Precious would think of his two new buddies. That should be an interesting introduction, he thought, as he swung his pack over his shoulder and headed into the school.

The Warriors were really glad to see him.

"Hey, Matt, what do you call these?" Jimmy Big Bear asked as he gingerly held one of Matt's miniscule braids out for everyone's inspection.

Matt flushed. "Even someone as un-cool as you should be able to figure that one out, Jimmy." He reached out and pulled the tiny braid out of his friend's big hand.

Geoff Starlight grinned. "Your new do is great, Matt. It's just missing one thing." He winked at Tony Manyponies. "Don't you think a warrior like Matt needs some special feathers to tie into those great braids?"

Tony nodded his head. "You're right, Geoff. Let's think, what would be an appropriate bird to get the feathers from? A fierce hawk or a swift falcon, or maybe a wise owl." He shook his head. "No, maybe not." His eyes twinkled as he nodded at Jimmy. "Can you think of a bird that might best represent our friend, Jimmy?"

"Let me think about that." Jimmy looked serious for a moment. "I know," he said finally, his face splitting into a huge grin, "a cute little chickadee!"

The others broke into good-natured laughter. Matt grinned, then had to laugh with his friends. After all, they were right. He was more of a chickadee than a hawk!

They asked how everything was going, including what he liked and didn't like about the Bandits' style of basketball.

Before he got a chance to answer, the doors from the change room opened and a tall, muscular boy with short, slicked-back hair came in. He immediately grabbed a basketball and started dribbling over toward them.

"Hi, I'm Jon Buffalo Runner. You must be Matt Eagletail. I've heard a lot of great things about you." He smiled and stuck out his hand for Matt to shake. Matt smiled back and shook his hand, a little taken aback at the guy's enthusiasm.

"Hi, Jon. I'd heard you were playing. Rumour has it you're pretty good, too." He nodded at the new player.

"Those kind of rumours I can handle." He grinned at Matt. "Here to watch?" he asked.

Matt felt awkward talking to this stranger about playing for his team.

"Actually, I thought I'd join you for a practice, you know, so I can keep up with the new plays. That way I'll be up to speed when I do come back."

The team members looked at one another uncomfortably, a couple of the guys cleared their throats self-consciously.

Matt looked from one face to another. "What's going on, Jimmy?" he asked, confused. He didn't like this. Suddenly he felt like he was really out of the loop.

"Actually, Matt, we've sort of, well, we replaced you in the starting lineup," Jimmy began explaining.

Matt thought about this. "I guess you have to until I come back," he said, nodding.

"No, not exactly," Jimmy continued. "We've replaced your position and Matt," he said slowly, "ah, we have a new captain, too."

Matt felt his stomach tighten up. He knew they'd have to get another point guard until he came back, but it sounded like they'd replaced him permanently.

"We know how much basketball means to you, Matt. We never expected you to put yourself on the shelf for us. That would be really unfair of us to ask." Jimmy's voice sounded odd to Matt, kind of choked. "We talked about it and decided that now that you have a new school and a new team, and knowing how important the game is to you, you'd naturally play for the Bandits. Who wouldn't, they're great! So we elected a new captain. We needed a team leader and Jon here," he said, nodding at Jon, who seemed okay with everything that was going on, "he's an awesome player and a super captain." Jimmy slapped the new captain on the back.

Jon just smiled and looked down at the floor self-consciously.

At least the guy who'd stolen his job had the good manners to look embarrassed at the lavish praise Jimmy was piling on him, Matt thought. He instantly felt bad for thinking something like that. Jon seemed like a good guy. It wasn't his fault.

Matt felt like he'd been punched in the stomach. He'd never expected this. It made him feel like the bottom had just fallen out of his world. He also had an odd feeling he couldn't put into words.

He tried to calm himself before he spoke. He swallowed. "Sure, I understand. Of course you moved on. I wasn't around, I can see why you needed a new point guard and," he said, his throat tight, "a new captain."

"You're still welcome to play with us, Matt. We can always use a sixth man like you, Cloud Leaper. No hard feelings?" Jimmy looked at his old friend and for the first time, Matt realized this was as hard for Jimmy as it was for him.

He smiled at his buddy. "None. Like you said, the game is all that's really important. I'll go change and you guys can show me how good the Warriors really are." He hoped the smile on his face didn't look as forced as it felt.

Matt went to change, then sat self-consciously on the bench watching as the guys he used to play with, hit the court. As he watched, he had to admit Jon was great. He had skill and power and a natural athletic agility which, coupled with his lightening speed, made him a force on the court.

He didn't seem to have any of the knack Matt did for predicting plays, but his genuine hustle and great shooting accuracy made up for it.

At the quarter, Jimmy insisted Matt get in on the action. He said they needed the competition of an ace player like Matt.

Once on the floor, the awkwardness Matt felt disappeared. He was home. He played for the squad opposing Jimmy's, where he worked hard enough to secure a tie by the time the final whistle went.

After the game, all the Warriors teased him good-naturedly, patting him on the back and saying how he hadn't lost his edge. They also said they missed him and hoped the Bandits knew what a lucky break they got having Matt Eagletail move to their school. Matt didn't say anything. It hadn't been the same playing with his team and he couldn't explain why.

By the time his mom came to pick him up later, he knew why it hadn't been the same. It had been tough saying goodbye to his teammates because this time, that's exactly what it did feel like. Matt wasn't a Warrior any more.

On the ride home, he listened to the twins chattering about their new pets as he stared out the window of the van. There was something peaceful and comforting about the way a field of tall grass waved slowly in the warm breeze. Never hurried, it was like a vast green ocean flowing forever across the gently rolling prairie.

"How was the game?" his mother asked, noticing his silence as she gave him a quick glance out of the corner of her eye.

"Okay. The Warriors have a new point guard." Matt was careful to keep his tone even. He continued to look out his side window.

"Oh," was all his mother said.

"And a new captain," he added, never shifting his gaze from the fields that were flashing by.

"Really," she said quietly.

"You were right, Mom. They are my friends." He suddenly realized what that odd feeling was he'd had earlier.

It was relief. He felt as though a weight had been lifted off his shoulders. He felt all the guilt he'd been having over playing with the Bandits disappear. The Warriors were his friends and they understood that things change whether you want them to or not. Like Jimmy said, they knew basketball was too important to Matt for them to expect him to stop playing because he couldn't play for the Warriors anymore, and Matt knew that was exactly it. He couldn't play for his old team anymore, but he didn't have to give up basketball. The iron knot that had been gripping his stomach untied itself and he suddenly felt better.

"Let's stop at the hardware store and see if they have a cage for the critters," he said, jerking his thumb back at the twins, who now had the cardboard box on the seat between them. He grinned mischievously. "Then maybe we'll see if they have one for the guinea pigs, too!"

"Sounds like a good idea," his mom agreed, ignoring Matt's lame joke.

"Then I'd really like to go home," Matt said, smiling at his mom.

She nodded and smiled too, keeping her eyes on the road.

11

Tryouts!

Point Guard: So, there you have it. I'm a man without a team. I may have to put my NBA plans on hold for a while until I get to high school and can get back into the game.

Free Throw: I'm sorry about the Warriors, Matt. But you have to look at it this way:

Now you're a free agent. You can play for any team you want!

Point Guard: I don't know what it's like where you are, but out here in the country, the choice of teams is pretty limited — like ONE.

Free Throw: SO ...

Point Guard: You don't understand. I already told Cory, the captain of the only team around, I wasn't interested. That option's not on the table.

Free Throw: What kind of an attitude is that?????? If you want to play for the Bandits, MAKE IT HAPPEN!!!!!!!!!! My granny always said — Can't is a Coward, Too Lazy to Work. If you want on this team, and we both know you do, then WORK for it, MAKE IT HAPPEN! Remember — YOU WIN IN YOUR HEAD FIRST!!!

Point Guard: Okay, okay, I get the point, stop shouting. Boy, subtlety sure isn't your strong point!

Free Throw: Where basketball is concerned, I take no prisoners!

Matt felt good as he signed off after chatting with Free Throw. The guy was right. If Matt wanted on the Bandits' team, he was going to have to find a way. As Free Throw had talked, Matt couldn't help but notice the similarity between his new best friend and his mother. They thought alike on a lot of things and they were usually right.

The walk home was a lot of fun that day. It turned out to be a real family affair.

"Hi, Mom, what are you doing here?" Matt asked as he, Jazz and the Geese walked out of the school doors and found his mom waiting with Precious. The two sets of twins were busy struggling into their backpacks.

"We expected just the usual escort," Jazz said, nodding at Precious, who sat wagging his huge plumy tail, sweeping a clean spot on the sidewalk as he did so.

"But we're glad you're here!" Marigold said, running over with Daisy and hugging Matt's mom fiercely.

"I'm happy you're here too," Violet interjected, not wanting to be left out.

"I wanted to talk to Matt about something," she said, smiling at them all as she rested her hand on the big white dog's head. "Let's get started and I'll explain."

As they made their way across the field toward home, all the girls busied themselves picking bouquets of wildflowers as Matt and his mom talked.

"I know how interested you've become in your roots and the history of the Tsuu T'ina people. I think that's really great." She smiled at her son.

"Actually, Mom, I'm finding some of the old stories and beliefs really fascinating. The Beaver people have some really interesting legends. I'm sure the Geese would love to hear some of them. They're a lot more interesting than anything Barney ever told them."

"Would you like to learn more about the Native way of life?" she asked. "Like how to build a birchbark canoe or a real teepee?"

Matt's eyes went wide. "Are you kidding? I'd love to. Does Grandpa have books on that stuff too?" he asked, an excited tone in his voice.

"Maybe, but what I have in mind is something else. Your stepdad and I have been doing some investigating and we think we've found the perfect answer for you." She continued, "There's a special school in Calgary called the Plains Indians Cultural Survival School. They specialize in teaching First Nations students about the way things were done in the old days — like teepees and canoes, but also the legends and language and way of life of past times. They have a class Saturday mornings you can go to." She paused. "What do you think?"

Matt knew saying yes would be a commitment, but it was one he was willing to make. He grinned at his mom. "Count me in."

His mom nodded, grinning back. "Great. I thought you'd want to give it a try. Classes start in the fall and you're already signed up. I think you're going to enjoy them."

"How'd you find out about this special school, Mom?" Matt asked, as they continued walking in the cool green shade.

"It was a team effort. I knew about the school, but your stepdad did all the research. He thought you might feel more at home if you didn't think you were losing everything about your First Nations life, just because you were no longer living on the reserve." She picked a piece of grass and held it between her thumbs, blowing into it to try and make a whistle.

"He's okay, this new husband of yours," Matt said, smiling at his mom.

"I think so," his mom agreed, smiling back.

* * *

That night Matt tried to think of a way he could approach Cory Cook for a chance to get on the Bandits. He couldn't ask Jazz to help him; she'd already done enough. She'd gone to a lot of trouble to open that door for him and he'd slammed it shut. Now he had to figure out how to open it again. The best approach is usually the most direct one, he decided. He'd talk to Cory after practice tomorrow and ask him for a spot on the team.

* * *

School dragged by the next day. Matt had decided his first priority now was to find himself a place on the Bandits. He was willing to ride the pine for the rest of this season, if that's what it took. He just wanted a chance to be on the team.

He could hardly wait to go to the gym and talk to Cory. Finally, the last bell rang and Matt grabbed his gear. He really wanted to be able to go on line and tell Free Throw he was now a Bragg Creek Bandit.

He walked into the gym and waited in the stands for Cory to show up. The rest of the team was already practising a lay-up drill when Cory finally came into the gym. He spotted Matt and waved. Matt waved back, but decided to wait where he was and talk to Cory after practice.

The practice was great to watch. The whole team played like a well-oiled machine. As Matt watched, he realized how much he'd missed the game. He really wanted to play.

After about fifteen minutes, there was a break in the drills and Cory walked over to Matt.

"Hey, Matt. This is weird that you're here." He took a long drink of his bottled water.

Matt thought he might be annoyed with him for the way he'd left the other day. He understood why the tall young captain would feel that way. Matt had been a jerk.

"Look, Cory, first let me say I'm sorry about the way I left the practice that day. You were great to give me a chance to play with the Bandits. I was ..." He hesitated, not knowing what to say.

"Don't sweat it," Cory said, interrupting him and waving his water bottle as if to dismiss the whole thing. "I talked to Jazz today and she explained you had a lot on your mind. I understand that." He nodded toward Matt's bag. "I don't suppose you've got your gym gear in there and feel like tossing a few balls around, do you?"

Matt smiled sheepishly. "As a matter of fact, I did bring my gear, and if you and the rest of the team don't mind, I'd really like to play."

Cory grinned at him. "Great! Today, you'll stay on my squad for the practice game!"

"You're on," Matt said, grabbing his pack and heading for the change rooms.

The next hour went by in a flash. Matt played point guard for Cory's squad and played most of the time. It was as if Cory wanted to see what Matt's limits were. Matt showed him he had no limits.

"Great game, Cloud Leaper," Cory said as they came off the court and started gathering their gear.

"Man, everyone was so hot today, you guys were dynamite!" Matt said, wiping the sweat from the back of his neck.

"I'd say everyone played first class, especially that short new guy," Cory said, laughing.

"Actually, Cory, I have something to ask you," Matt began awkwardly. He felt really strange, but took a deep breath and went on. "I know it's late in the season and everything, but I was wondering, if you have an opening or need a spare man, would you consider me for the spot?" He could feel his face burning. *The best approach is usually the most direct one.* Who's brilliant idea had that been, he wondered?

"Matt, I know you can play, and I know the guys think you're great." He nodded seriously at Matt, his eyes not betraying anything. "Look," he said frowning, pursing his lips, "our lineup's pretty well set, but let me think it over and I'll let you know."

Matt thought Cory was acting a little weird, but accepted the captain's decision.

"Sure, Cory," he said, trying not to show how disappointed he felt. "That would be great. Even if it doesn't work out for this year, I'd like the chance to play next year." Matt picked up his pack. "And thanks for the practice." He started across the gym, but when he glanced back at Cory, the Bandit captain was still watching Matt and now he was grinning.

* * *

When Matt walked in the backdoor, Jazz was lying on the floor, with her feet up on the couch where Precious lay sound asleep.

"Hi, Matt, there's a message for you on the answering machine," she called, waggling her feet at him.

Matt raced upstairs to the kitchen, which is where the machine was. He hit the replay button. Cory's voice spoke to him.

"Hi, Matt. I know this is short notice and all, but the Bandits have a problem we were hoping you'd be able to help us out with." Matt listened, curious and a little confused. Cory hadn't said anything about a problem.

He listened as Cory's message continued. "You remember when you were sixth man for us because one of our players was cut? The truth is, we have a big hole on the Bandits' starting lineup, which we haven't been able to fill. With a shot at the championship coming up, we really need a good point guard. Do you know anyone who could help us out? If you do, could he come back to the gym this afternoon? We're having a practice and we'll work the guy in." Matt could hear the smile in Cory's voice.

No wonder he'd acted so weird this afternoon. He'd obviously left the message just before coming to the gym, where Matt was waiting.

"YES!" Matt yelled excitedly. This was great. He was going to be a Bandit! He was going to get to play again!

Wait till Free Throw hears about this, he thought, heading downstairs to tell Jazz.

When he got downstairs, Jazz was grinning from ear to ear. "What's new?" she asked innocently, then burst out giggling. "Cory called just before you got home and told me what had happened. I think it's hysterical. Talk about crossed communication."

Matt shrugged his shoulders about the mix-up, grinning. "As long as everyone's on the same wavelength now and I get to play for the Bandits, who cares?"

12

Mixed Loyalties

Free Throw: You are AWESOME!!! I knew you'd do it.

Point Guard: Well, I'm glad one of us did. I guess I just needed someone to give me a shove. If I'd waited, it would have been too late. I found out later from Jazz, who can't keep a secret, that there was one other guy they were considering for the position, but after playing with me, Cory had his heart set on yours truly. If I hadn't been so, you know, rigidly set in my ways, shall we say, I could have been playing for the Bandits a lot sooner.

Free Throw: I guess this means your plan for a NBA career is back on track.

Point Guard: OUR NBA careers are back on track. We've been dreaming of playing in the big league, and you just about had to leave me behind. Funny how things work out.

Free Throw: And speaking of working out, it sounds like the new improved Point Guard family is doing okay.

Point Guard: Better than okay. The Geese have finally decided their guinea pigs are more fun to be around than I am. I bet they haven't asked me more than five questions in the last week, which is making my life a lot simpler.

Free Throw: That should give you more time to concentrate on the important things in life — like PM-ing me every little detail about your new team!

Matt grinned as he signed off. Free Throw was so squir-relly, Matt was sure his friend would have no trouble living in Matt's world.

* * *

Over the next two weeks, the Bandits won three important games and Matt played in all of them. With their last win, the Bandits had clinched a spot in the Foothills Zone Champion-ship, which would be played on the following Saturday. The excitement was growing as everyone waited to see who the Bandits would be playing against. The team was unstoppable and everyone's spirits were way up. The whole school had Championship fever.

Matt was beginning to feel like his world was coming together again. He'd started to get to know some of the guys on the team and had even gone over to their houses to play video games or just hang out.

When the phone rang, Matt picked it up and was happily surprised to hear Cory's voice on the other end.

"Hey, Matt, how's it going?" Cory asked conversationally.

"Just fine, my little stepsisters are all over at friends' so it's peaceful for a half-hour. What's up?" Matt asked as he flopped down on the family room couch.

"Actually, I just got some news and I thought I'd call you myself and let you know." Cory's voice sounded strained and Matt instantly wondered what was wrong.

"Cory, what news?" he asked, apprehension beginning to form a knot in his stomach. Had something happened to one of the Bandits?

"I just heard who we're going to play against in the Zone Championship Saturday." There was a pause at the other end.

Matt waited.

Cory cleared his throat and went on. "Matt, we're playing the Tsuu T'ina Warriors. I thought I'd better call you before you heard it through the grapevine. Are you going to be okay with this? I know you have a history with the team."

Matt sat in stunned silence. He knew the Warriors had been doing well, but with the hectic schedule the past two weeks, he hadn't called Jimmy to see where they were in the standings. The Bandits against the Warriors. Matt didn't know what to say.

"Look, Matt, I know this is going to be hard for you, but, as captain of the Bandits, I need to know where you stand. If you don't think you can do this, I need to know now."

Matt felt all mixed up inside. He'd always known it was possible that the Bandits would play against the Warriors, but he'd never really thought about it.

This was the Zone Championship. This had been the Warriors' goal since Matt had started playing for the team. This was the year they were going all the way, and they had. But Matt wasn't going to be playing for them when they went for their ultimate goal, and worse, he was going to be playing for the team that could take the Championship away.

Because, Matt realized, that's what could happen. He knew the Warriors were good, but he now knew what an awesome team the Bandits were. If he played for the Bandits, he could be helping them defeat his old team.

But Cory had stood by him, given him a chance to play. Cory was counting on him to play 100 percent for the Bandits. He couldn't let his new team or his new friend down.

"Don't worry, Cory. I'm a Bandit now and as a Bandit, I'm telling you our team is going to win the Zone Championship this weekend." He hoped he sounded surer of himself than he felt. His stomach was doing flip-flops. He knew Cory understood what this meant to him. It had been hard for Matt to give up on the idea of going back to the Warriors and even harder for him to go to another team. But anyone who loves basketball knows it's playing that's important and Matt desperately wanted to play.

"Matt, I knew I could count on you. We're going to need Cloud Leaper on Saturday and I wasn't looking forward to playing without him."

Matt hung up the phone still feeling a little weak in the knees. But he'd made a commitment to Cory and he was going to stick by it. He just hoped the Warriors would understand — this was basketball.

* * *

Saturday morning began with a bang.

"Matty! Matty! Wake up!" all four twins screamed as they slammed open his bedroom door.

Matt pulled the pillow over his head. Marigold and Daisy jumped on the bed and began relentlessly pulling at his pillow.

"You have to get up! We have a four-alarm emergency!" Violet yelled.

"What?" Matt mumbled, not willing to open his eyes until the exact nature of the emergency was made clear to him.

"They're gone!" Rosemary wailed.

"Who are gone?" Matt asked.

"Guinevere and Arthur!" all four twins shouted in unison.

"You have to get up and help us find them," Daisy said, helpfully reaching for his housecoat. "Come on, we haven't a moment to lose. If Mom starts vacuuming, they could get sucked up and be gone *forever*!" Her face looked so deadly serious, it was all Matt could do not to laugh.

Groaning, he knew his sleeping time had come to an end. "Okay, but you all have to leave while I get dressed. You four go start searching the family room and ..." — he tried to put this delicately, not wanting to frighten the girls — "put Precious outside." He knew if the big dog saw two guinea pigs scurrying across the carpet, he'd have no choice but to hunt them down. It's what dogs did!

After more than an hour of searching, the two guinea pigs were eventually found hiding in the bottom of an old pyjama bag, but Arthur and Guinevere had a surprise for the Thoreau-Eagletail family. There were now four baby guinea pigs, much to the delight of Marigold, Daisy, Violet and Rosemary.

Matt left the family discussing what was to be done with the new expanded rodent population and went outside to the basketball hoop. The early-morning sun felt good on his face as he stood and looked at the net. Grabbing the ball, he decided a little pre-game practice was just what he needed.

Jimmy had called the night before to talk about the upcoming game. He'd reassured Matt that he understood about his playing against the Warriors. He was great about it and had even said he was looking forward to winning. He hoped there'd be no hard feelings when the Warriors took the cup home without Matt's name on it.

Matt had felt better after he'd hung up with Jimmy, but he was still more nervous over this game than any other he'd played in his life. His stomach was doing 360-degree loops.

"Are you going to be okay today?" Jazz asked quietly as she closed the screen door behind her. She had understood how hard today's game was going to be for him.

"Yeah, I think I will be," Matt said, still staring at the basketball hoop. "It's just hard to wrap my head around the fact that I worked my butt off the past three years to get the Warriors a shot at the championship, and now, I'm playing against them. It's going to be strange not passing to a Warrior player and to a Bandit instead."

Jazz nodded. "I can see why you're a little freaked out. But I have faith in you. You're going to play so great today, the Eagletail name will live forever in the Bragg Creek Bandits hall of fame." She looked at her stepbrother, understanding.

Matt sighed. "I was just thinking about everything that's happened over the last while." He grabbed the basketball from where it lay against the garage wall, took aim and dropped a perfect set shot into the net. "You know, all the changes and everything."

Jazz grabbed the ball as it bounced back toward them. "Would you say the changes are mostly good or mostly bad?" she asked, sending an off shot toward the net herself.

"I guess mostly," Matt began, then paused, grabbing the rebound from her unsuccessful attempt, "good." He smiled at Jazz, who nodded and smiled back. They played in companionable silence for a long while.

That was one thing he liked about his new stepsister. She knew when not to talk.

13

Some Win, Some Lose

Matt slammed through the doors to the school, his gym bag slapping his back as he ran. He was late and he knew it. Of all the bad timing …

He could hear the crowd in the gym applauding as the Warriors and Bandits warmed up. He should be on the floor with them now! Up ahead he spotted Jazz at the change room doors and he knew she was waiting for him. He could see she was fuming.

"I know, I know, Jazz," he said, waving off her reprimand before she could voice it. "I was held up." He grinned sheepishly at his stepsister, who was staring at him, open-mouthed. He was sporting a new, very short hairdo.

She exhaled loudly, then relaxed and grinned at him. "You look great!" was all she said.

He felt his face grow hot. "I didn't think cutting off two little braids would take so long," he said self-consciously as he ran his hand through his freshly cropped hair.

Jazz continued to give him an inquiring look.

He could see she wanted an explanation for the big change. "It's like this," Matt began awkwardly. "I thought about everything that's happened and decided I don't have to grow my hair out in braids or live on the reserve to remind myself I am First Nations. I know in my heart where my roots are and I'm proud of my ancestors and their history. I don't have anything to prove and I have nothing to forget." He might have sounded like a geek, but that was how he felt.

Jazz simply nodded and smiled, understanding what he was trying to say. Matt was amazed at how easily she could do just that — understand how he felt without making a big deal out of it.

He smiled back at her, then nodded toward the gym. "I'd better hustle. Can you tell Cory I'm just getting suited up?" he asked, as he started toward the change room door.

"Wait!" Jazz exclaimed, excitedly grabbing his arm. "I've got you something."

It was then Matt noticed the package wrapped in brightly coloured birthday paper Jazz had under her arm. "Here, happy birthday!" She grinned at him and handed him the present.

"But it's not my birthday," Matt said, confused.

"Just open it, Hot Shot," she giggled.

Matt tore open the wrapper and grinned. Inside was a purple and gold Bragg Creek Bandits jersey with a large number 1 displayed proudly.

"It's Muggsy Bogues's number," she said, obviously proud of herself. "I checked with the rest of the team and they thought since you couldn't wear your Tsuu T'ina Warrior number, perhaps the famous Golden State Warriors was a good choice for you." Jazz was beaming at him. "Cool, huh?"

"Cool," Matt agreed. "We can't lose now. This is the best present I've ever had. Thanks, Jazz." He grinned gratefully at his stepsister and headed for the change room.

* * *

The gymnasium was hopping by the time Matt hit the floor. He had no idea this many people would turn out for the game. Sure it was the Foothills Zone Championship and he knew the Bragg Creek fans would be out supporting their team, but since the game was being played way out here in the Creek, he hadn't expected so many people from Calgary. He looked around the stands for his family and he realized that he *did* think of them as his family.

Matt smiled and waved when he saw them. They'd have been hard to miss, even if they hadn't had a large white dog with a bandanna in Bandits' colours tied around his neck sitting with them.

The whistle blew and both teams formed up for the opening tip-off.

Matt looked around at all the familiar faces on both teams. It felt really strange to see the Warriors form up at the jump circle with him and know he was playing for a different team.

Jimmy Big Bear, who played small forward, caught his eye and gave him the thumbs-up signal. Matt nodded and smiled at his friend. He looked at the other Warriors, expecting to see anger or disgust, but instead he saw smiles and nods of approval. These guys were truly his friends and they understood — the game was everything. Matt took a deep breath and returned his attention to the ref, who held the ball. It was going to be a wicked game.

From the first seconds of the game, it was high-voltage, non-stop action.

Everyone, on both teams, was playing at a level higher than they had all year.

The ref's whistle had barely stopped echoing before the crowd was treated to some really excellent passing from the Bandits. Cory, an inspiration to the rest of the team, started with a roar as he won the opening tip-off from Geoff Starlight, the Warriors' centre. The Bandits' ball was tipped to Bruce O'Conner, the power forward, then snapped to Ron Klassen, the small forward, who took it home for the first basket of the game.

The hometown fans went wild as the auditorium erupted in a storm of cheers and whistles.

Matt had at first thought he'd have an unfair advantage over the Warriors because he'd played with them for so long and knew their moves. The next few plays soon proved him wrong as Jimmy repeatedly anticipated Matt's next move because he knew also how Matt would play. Matt tried to be careful not to telegraph what he was going to do.

As he watched the ball being worked down court toward him, Matt could feel his heart pounding in his chest. The adrenaline rush he always got in a game was starting to pump Matt up. He might be an ex-Warrior, but he was also a Bandit, one who wanted to win. He seemed to run at 110 percent when he was in an actual game. He could see clearer and think faster. That was how he was able to anticipate the other team's moves. His *sixth sense* was what Jimmy had always called it and Matt could feel it cranking up.

Jon Buffalo Runner, the point guard, expertly moved the ball into shooting range, then with a lightening quick move, drove into the paint and went up for a beautiful hook shot. The *sky-hook* swished home.

The Warrior fans hooted their approval.

Once the play was in the lane, instinct usually took over for most of the players. Your reflexes and automatic responses were what scored baskets in the crush under the net. Great rebounding was essential, but first the shooter had to miss and with a hot hand like Jon, Matt knew the Bandits were in for a fight.

The passes continued to be crisp and bullet fast; the shots were dead on the mark and the speed of the game seemed accelerated. The players were always moving — running, jumping or dodging, except for that split second when the ball hung in the air, as if suspended, before hitting the basket.

Matt loved the fast pace of the game. Mark Fox, the Warriors' shooting guard had just inbounded the ball to Tony Manyponies, their power forward, when Matt glanced around at the other Warrior players. He suddenly knew what they were going to do and started over to Jon Buffalo Runner.

"Cory," Matt called, "you and Ron, cover their small forward. He's going to be passed the ball, then cut to the weak side before he smokes in for a lay-up."

Cory and Ron both hesitated a fraction of a second, then they converged on Jimmy Big Bear. Matt continued shadowing Jon, who now had possession.

Matt had called it. The Warriors tried working the ball so Jimmy could take a pass, but Cory and Ron had him too well covered.

Matt swooped in and scooped the ball as Jon tried to get a shot off to Jimmy.

Instantly turning for the far net, Matt wove expertly through traffic, loving the way the ball seemed to be attached to his hand like a yo-yo on a string. Breaking out, he flew down the undefended court and soared in for a perfect lay-up.

He grinned to himself. He was what the sports reporters would call a *snowbird*, a real Canadian Snowbird.

The first-quarter score was Bandits 14, Warriors 8.

The crowd was cheering and Matt felt elated.

This feeling faded a little as he moved back to cover his man for the next play. As Matt ran past the Warriors, he could see the looks of steely determination on their faces. He knew that look. They were going to push harder. They were going to push the limits to take the lead. The game was about to click into a higher gear and the Bandits had no idea what they were in for.

When the whistle blew to start the second quarter, the Warriors stormed onto the floor like they were on fire. It was as if they were making up for not being in the playoffs all those other years. They were a big, strong team who went after the lead like a bunch of steamrollers.

The sweat was running off Matt as the whole team hustled harder and faster to try and stop their determined rivals. The Warriors burned up the court with pass after pass and basket after basket.

They'd become unstoppable. Every Bandit redoubled their efforts, but it just wasn't working. Glancing at the scoreboard, Matt could see his old team's determination reflected in the ever-increasing Warrior score.

Matt re-focused. He watched as Mark Fox, using his larger size to out-muscle his opponent, stole the ball from Larry Chang, the Bandits' shooting guard. Mark started zig-zagging his way toward the net. Matt knew he was going to try a long lob. He had the strength for it; his arms were all muscles.

Too far away to stop it, Matt yelled at Bruce O'Conner, who was the closest man to Mark. "Bruce, he's going for the long bomb!" But before Bruce could move into position to block the attempt, Mark pulled the ball into his chest and sent it flying in a high, graceful arc. Swish!

Matt heard the groans from his Bandit teammates. The Warriors' lead was growing.

The Bandits seemed to be losing confidence as fast as they were losing ground.

As the halftime whistle shrilled, the score was a commanding 36-20, for the Warriors.

Matt knew the Bandits were going to have to really work in the second half to overcome the killer lead the Warriors now had.

* * *

The size difference between the Warriors and the Bandits had suddenly become a real factor in the game. Matt was still the shortest player on the Bandits, if only by a few inches. But when he stood with his old teammates on the Warriors, he was considerably smaller than any of them. The Warriors were a big bunch of guys and they weren't afraid to use this to their advantage.

It didn't matter to Matt, who'd played with these bigger guys his whole basketball life, but a lot of the Bandits were having trouble adjusting to the aggressive style of play the Warriors were using so well. Matt headed to the bench. He listened as the coach went over some plays and tried to get the team back into the right frame of mind.

Matt knew the Bandits were feeling like they'd lost already and that attitude was a sure way to make it happen. He took a long drink from his water bottle and hoped his teammates wouldn't take what he had to say the wrong way.

"Okay, guys, I know I'm the new player on the team, but can I offer a little teammate advice?" He had their attention. "You've got to stop looking at those guys as unbeatable just because they're bigger than us. That wasn't a factor when we started this game and it shouldn't shut us down now." He glanced around at each of them. "I've been playing bigger guys my whole life and I've never let it affect me except to make me try harder." He had to get through to them. He thought of how he sometimes imagined himself a Snowbird jet pilot. "Sure we're smaller than most of the Warriors, but we're also faster and more manoeuvrable. Think of us as F-16 fighter jets and they're B-52 bombers. Bigger bang for the buck, sure, but we can fly circles around them." He paused and took a deep breath. "A friend once told me something I'll never forget — *you win in your head first!* We're winners. The

Warriors just don't know it yet, so let's go show them. And remember," he said, grinning at his teammates, "think F-16's!" Matt knew it was an odd comparison, but he had to do something to stop the downward spiral his team was on. *You win in your head first!*

His talk did the trick. The team began chanting *F-16's, F-16's* as they noisily jostled and high-fived each other. When they headed back out onto the floor, even the crowd knew something was different.

Matt soon had the opportunity to show his old teammates that the Cloud Leaper was not going to let a little point spread keep him down.

Moving to the circle, he grinned at a surprised Jon Buffalo Runner, who stood opposite him. Matt could see in Jon's face that he didn't consider Matt real competition for the jump ball. That was okay with Matt.

The second the ref tossed the ball, he tensed his legs and, waiting for exactly the right second, jumped. Jon never knew what hit him. Matt easily won the tip-off, tapping it to Larry Chang, who snagged it, pulled it in to his chest and pivoted.

"Cloud Leaper!" Larry called, passing the ball back to Matt and setting up a screen in the Bandits' own version of a give-and-go. "Go deep!" He grinned at Matt, who dodged around Geoff Starlight and headed to a small open spot on the strong side of the court.

"Cory," Matt called, nodding to the Bandit captain, who figured out at once what Matt wanted him to do. The tall centre headed down court.

Matt dribbled into the Warriors' end with lightening speed, then cut behind Cory, who was setting a pick for him and went in for a perfect two point lay-up! The crowd cheered.

The Warriors inbounded the ball and started down the court like they owned it. Cory signalled to Larry and Matt, the two guards, who got ready to intercept Geoff Starlight as he moved toward the Bandits' net.

As the two Bandit players approached, they suddenly threw their arms up and started waving like they were trying to block any possible pass or shot Geoff might be thinking of making.

Geoff momentarily hesitated. That was all it took for Matt to smack the ball over to Larry, who grabbed it, and snapped a hard chest pass to Cory, who took it home! Two more points!

The team's attitude was now one of winners in waiting. Everyone doubled their efforts and everywhere on the court you could hear the Bandits' code word for victory — *F-16's F-16's*. It wasn't long before the crowd took up the call and soon the whole gymnasium was chanting along with the Bandit players.

By the fourth quarter, the Warriors' scoring drive had been drastically reduced, but they weren't giving up the lead without a fight.

Matt could see the determined look on Jimmy's face as he took an inbound ball and started dribbling toward the waiting Bandits.

"Okay, let's take it to them!" Matt called and started forward to intercept Jimmy.

The Bandits moved out like a swarm of mad hornets. They moved around and through the Warriors, never staying still long enough for their opponents to get a fix on them.

Ron Klassen suddenly stopped his erratic movement and began moving around Jimmy in a tight circle, almost, but never touching the big Warrior forward. Jimmy began concentrating on avoiding Ron's attempts to snag the ball.

This was Matt's cue. He streaked in, blindsiding Jimmy. Scooping the ball, he snapped a hard bounce pass to Bruce, who headed down court. Tony and Jimmy started after him, but they were too late. Nothing but net!

The crowd cheered like it was the winning basket in a NBA playoff game!

As the final minutes of the game began, the score remained 60-56 for the aggressive Tsuu T'ina team.

With the clock ticking down, Ron Klassen managed a break away and headed down court with a pack of Warriors hot on his heels. Looking for help, he spotted Cory in the clear on the weak side. After a brilliant pump fake, which caught Tony Manyponies off guard, Ron did a three-sixty and sent a perfect overhead pass to Cory.

Cory eyed the basket, then went straight up and, with really impressive hang time, fired from 13 feet out! Swish! It was good! The crowd erupted in cheers! 60-58! The Bandits weren't out of it yet!

With only a couple of minutes left, the Warriors knew all they had to do was kill the clock and they'd win the Championship.

Matt glanced at the fans. None of them were quitting on their team and Matt hoped none of the Bandits were quitting on their fans. He saw his family in the stands; his parents were cheering and all the twins were stamping their feet and blowing their noisemakers. When he spotted Jazz, she waved and yelled, "*Go Cloud Leaper.*"

As the ball was thrown in, Matt could see the Warriors weren't going to let any Bandits get near enough to take possession. They headed toward the Bandits' basket with a wall of players protecting the ball. The clock was ticking.

The Bandits not only had to get the ball, they had to score twice in less than two minutes to win this game.

"Full court press!" Matt called and all the Bandits rushed the Warriors, stopping their advance. Jon Buffalo Runner had possession and his ball control was very impressive. He continued to play keep away with the Bandit players.

None of the Bandits could get close enough to try for a turnover.

Matt watched the play for a second, then knew what he had to do. "Cory, force a pass," he called.

Cory, with a quick glance at everyone's position, nodded.

Matt just hoped Cory's forced pass was to the right player.

Using Ron Klassen, the small forward, as a screen, Matt waited until Cory moved in, pressing Jon toward Ron's position.

The tall Warrior captain pivoted and, keeping one arm out to block Ron, launched a high hook shot to Tony Manyponies, who was conveniently in the clear.

Matt could hear his blood pounding in his ears as he darted out from behind Ron and, gathering himself for the spring, leapt into the air.

He intercepted the ball at the height of its arc. Coming down hard, Matt pivoted, and, taking in the situation at a glance, realized he had no where to go. There were Warriors everywhere. Low dribbling, he dodged Geoff Starlight and squeaked past Jimmy Big Bear.

Matt headed out away from the Warriors' basket, crossing the three-point line.

The crowd was counting down the clock. Five, four, three …

Matt had no choice. Turning, he eyed the basket. It looked *very* far away.

Pulling the ball into his hip and lowering himself into a semi-crouch, he gathered all the strength he had and, keeping his eye on the inside rim of the basket, fired.

The ball, looking like it was moving in slow motion, arced high and long. Matt's heart was pounding so loudly, he only half heard the final buzzer sound.

He held his breath as the ball came down.

The ref's arm was up, acknowledging Matt's attempt, then his other arm went up signifying a successful three-point basket! Even in the NBA, a Hail Mary from that far downtown would have been front-page news!

Matt couldn't believe it! He'd done it. They'd won — Bandits 61, Warriors 60.

The team ran to him and picked him up, carrying him on their shoulders to the bench. Everyone was laughing and yelling so hard, he was powerless to stop them. The auditorium was vibrating from the fans screaming and stomping their feet. This was a win to savour!

All the Bandits were slapping him on the back and pouring water over his head from their water bottles at the bench. Matt just grinned.

Even with all the yelling, shouting and congratulations, he couldn't help but think about how the Warriors must be feeling. They'd fought hard and had nearly won. It had been a game neither team would ever forget.

Looking over at the Warrior bench, Matt caught Jimmy's eye. He gave his old friend a thumbs-up. Jimmy looked back at Matt for a long moment. Then, shrugging his shoulders and grinning wearily at Matt, returned the signal. Matt nodded his head and smiled back. It was okay. He sighed with relief, realizing how much it meant to him to still be able to call the Warriors his friends.

Suddenly, a thought popped into Matt's head. *Wait till Free Throw hears about this!* He grinned to himself, anticipating his cyber-friend's reaction. Life really was great!

* * *

Both teams had gone out to celebrate and it had turned into a very noisy, happy affair. Highlights of the game were rehashed, with particular emphasis on the star of the game and his three-point wonder. The Warriors were very good losers. They vowed to be back next year and win! Matt felt good sitting with all his friends from both teams and retelling basketball stories about near wins and losses.

One thing everyone agreed on, Matt had a NBA career waiting for him in the future.

When, after twice as much pizza as usual had been demolished, the two teams broke the party up, Matt happily climbed into the family van and, finally, started to relax.

The twins giggled all the way home and if Matt hadn't been so tired, he would have quizzed them as to what new evil they'd done.

When they pulled into the driveway, Precious was the first out of the van. He bounded across the freshly re-sodded lawn and started scratching at the back door.

"Okay, okay, we're coming," Matt called.

"Matt, would you go open the door?" his mother asked as she began unloading the two smallest twins.

"Sure, Mom," he said, taking the keys she offered him.

He walked to the back door, his bag of gym clothes over his shoulder. Fumbling a little with the key, he barely got the door open before the eager dog surged forward into the basement.

Matt followed, his hand looking for the light switch to brighten the early evening shadows.

He flipped the switch on and stopped.

"Surprise!" came a chorus of voices behind him.

Matt stood staring at a complete home computer system including a 17-inch monitor, speakers, fax, printer and scanner!

It was wonderful!

He stared, not knowing what this was all about.

His stepdad spoke up. "We decided since you were so interested in computers and the Internet, it made more sense for you to have one at home so you could talk to your friend any time you wanted to." He smiled at Matt.

"And," his mother said, grinning, "Gordon's boss has said he can telecommute twice a week, which means he'll be home a lot more." She put an arm around her husband's waist. "I think it's brilliant! The whole family can use it."

"Can we play games?" Marigold asked.

"Can we go to all those zoomy Web sites we hear about on TV?" Rosemary asked.

"I want to play games too," Daisy wailed.

"Stop blubbering, you baby," Jazz said. "You don't even know how to turn it on yet." She rolled her eyes. "Geese!"

Matt laughed. "This is some surprise. It's going to be great." He smiled at the twins. "You can play games on it, but it's not just a toy. You can use it to find out lots of information on strange people and places and all kinds of things you always wondered about. Oh, and I guess you could use it for schoolwork too." He grinned at his parents. "By the time you girls go to university, you'll be the most computer-literate geese in Bragg Creek."

"Well, don't just stand there — go crank it up!" his mother admonished, giving him a gentle shove toward the waiting machine.

Matt headed over to the new Pentium II. He turned it on and was happy to see that he recognized some of the same icons that the school computers had. Hitting the Internet access picture, he waited as the machine buzzed and clicked, making its connection to the World Wide Web.

He signed on and worked his way to the usual NBA chat room, hoping Free Throw was on line. As soon as he signed in to the chat room, he was rewarded by several people telling him Free Throw was just there and had left a message for Point Guard to PM him at 5:00, MDT.

Matt glanced down at the time showing in the lower right hand corner of the screen. It was just about 5:00 now.

Suddenly, the message box that said who was in the chat room winked a new arrival. Free Throw was in the room.

Matt quickly typed in a greeting and then he and Free Throw left the public room to chat privately.

Free Throw: So — am I in the presence of a champ?

Point Guard: I can only hope a NBA scout was sitting in the stands watching the way we kicked Warrior butt today!!!!!

Free Throw: CONGRATS!!!! This is news I like. I can already see your name on the team roster of the Vancouver Grizzlies!

Point Guard: Maybe OUR names on the same roster, that would be something for both of us to work for, buddy! You and I on the same team — that would be great! What do you say?

Matt waited for Free Throw to agree. It was a dream they could both shoot for. He knew his friend loved the game as much as he did. The screen remained blank. Matt wondered what was keeping his friend's reply. Then a message came through.

Free Throw: Point Guard, there's something I have to tell you. First, my real name is John Salton and I live in San Francisco, California. Second, I can never play in the NBA because two years ago I was in an automobile accident that left me paralyzed from the waist down. I get around in an electric wheelchair and will never walk again, let alone play basketball.

Matt stared at the screen, re-reading the message. He didn't know what to say. Free Throw was the biggest basketball fan he knew, besides himself. Why hadn't he told him this before? How could he be so enthusiastic about the game when he could never play it? Matt pushed his chair away from the keyboard, feeling suddenly awkward and at a loss for words.

His mother laid her hand on his shoulder. "Aren't you going to answer him, Matt?" she asked softly.

Matt looked up at his mother. He could feel his face grow hot. "What am I supposed to say? The guy's been lying to me all this time."

"Has he, Matt? Was he lying when he said he lived for basketball just like you do or when he told you about his favourite players or encouraged you to do the one thing you loved to do — play basketball?"

Matt suddenly felt embarrassed. He swallowed the lump that had formed in his throat. His mom was right. The guy on the other end of this computer was still his best friend, Free Throw. That was the important thing. He rolled his chair up to the keyboard.

Point Guard: Okay, so you'll never PLAY in the NBA, but the game needs great COACHES just as much as great players. You'll be my coach on the Vancouver Grizzlies when I play. Hey, have you given any thought to a wheelchair team? I've seen some of those guys play and they're AWESOME! By the way, my name is Matt Eagletail and I live in a small town in Alberta called Bragg Creek.

He waited for a reply, unsure of how his friend would respond. The screen suddenly flashed.

Free Throw: Matt, we can talk about the wheelchair basketball later. It's not out of the question. Right now, I want to get one thing clear, so there'll be no misunderstanding ...

Matt tensed, waiting to read what his friend would say next. The cursor began moving.

Free Throw: I hope you're not expecting any special treatment at training camp, just because you're my BEST FRIEND.

As if on cue, his mom said, "Okay, ladies, let's give Matt a little elbow room while he talks to his friend." To a general chorus of groans, she ushered the girls upstairs with his stepdad following behind, herding the grumbling Geese ahead of him.

Ignoring the hubbub, Matt went back to the keyboard.

Point Guard: As my prospective coach, you're going to love this ... Take a wild guess who sunk a perfect three-pointer to win the championship game today?

Matt smiled to himself as he watched the computer screen, waiting for his friend's reply.

Other books you'll enjoy in the Sports Stories series...

Baseball

☐ *Curve Ball* by John Danakas #1
Tom Poulos is looking forward to a summer of baseball in Toronto until his mother puts him on a plane to Winnipeg.

☐ *Baseball Crazy* by Martyn Godfrey #10
Rob Carter wins an all-expenses-paid chance to be batboy at the Blue Jays' spring training camp in Florida.

☐ *Shark Attack* by Judi Peers #25
The East City Sharks have a good chance of winning the county championship until their arch rivals get a tough new pitcher.

Basketball

☐ *Fast Break* by Michael Coldwell #8
Moving from Toronto to small-town Nova Scotia was rough, but when Jeff makes the school basketball team he thinks things are looking up.

☐ *Camp All-Star* by Michael Coldwell #12
In this insider's view of a basketball camp, Jeff Lang encounters some unexpected challenges.

☐ *Nothing but Net* by Michael Coldwell #18
The Cape Breton Grizzly Bears face an out-of-town basketball tournament they're sure to lose.

☐ *Slam Dunk* by Steven Barwin and Gabriel David Tick #23
In this sequel to *Roller Hockey Blues*, Mason Ashbury's basketball team adjusts to the arrival of some new players: girls.

☐ *Courage on the Line* by Cynthia Bates #33
After Amelie changes schools, she must confront difficult former teammates in an extramural match.

Figure Skating

☐ *A Stroke of Luck* by Kathryn Ellis #6
Strange accidents are stalking one of the skaters at the Millwood Arena.

☐ *The Winning Edge* by Michele Martin Bosley #28
Jennie wants more than anything to win a grueling series of competitions, but is success worth losing her friends?

Gymnastics

☐ *The Perfect Gymnast* by Michele Martin Bossley #9
Abby's new friend has all the confidence she needs, but she also has a serious problem that nobody but Abby seems to know about.

Ice Hockey

☐ *Two Minutes for Roughing* by Joseph Romain #2
As a new player on a tough Toronto hockey team, Les must fight to fit in.

☐ *Hockey Night in Transcona* by John Danakas #7
Cody Powell gets promoted to the Transcona Sharks' first line, bumping out the coach's son who's not happy with the change.

☐ *Face Off* by C.A. Forsyth #13
A talented hockey player finds himself competing with his best friend for a spot on a select team.

☐ *Hat Trick* by Jacqueline Guest #20
The only girl on an all-boys' hockey team works to earn the captain's respect and her mother's approval.

☐ *Hockey Heroes* by John Danakas #22
A left-winger on the thirteen-year-old Transcona Sharks adjusts to a new best friend and his mom's boyfriend.

☐ *Hockey Heat Wave* by C.A. Forsyth #27
In this sequel to *Face Off*, Zack and Mitch encounter some trouble when it looks like only one of them will make the select team at hockey camp.

☐ *Shoot to Score* by Sandra Richmond #31
Playing defence on the B list, alongside the coach's mean-spirited son, are tough obstacles for Steven to overcome, but he perseveres and changes his luck.

Riding
☐ *A Way With Horses* by Peter McPhee #11
A young Alberta rider invited to study show jumping at a posh local riding school uncovers a secret.

☐ *Riding Scared* by Marion Crook #15
A reluctant new rider struggles to overcome her fear of horses.

☐ *Katie's Midnight Ride* by C.A. Forsyth #16
An ambitious barrel racer finds herself without a horse weeks before her biggest rodeo.

☐ *Glory Ride* by Tamara L. Williams #21
Chloe Anderson fights memories of a tragic fall for a place on the Ontario Young Riders' Team.

☐ *Cutting it Close* by Marion Crook #24
In this novel about barrel racing, a talented young rider finds her horse is in trouble just as she is about to compete in an important event.

Roller Hockey
☐ *Roller Hockey Blues* by Steven Barwin and Gabriel David Tick #17
Mason Ashbury faces a summer of boredom until he makes the roller-hockey team.

Running
☐ *Fast Finish* by Bill Swan #30
Noah is a promising young runner headed for the provincial finals when he suddenly decides to withdraw from the event.

Sailing

☐ *Sink or Swim* by William Pasnak #5
Dario can barely manage the dog paddle, but thanks to his mother he's spending the summer at a water sports camp.

Soccer

☐ *Lizzie's Soccer Showdown* by John Danakas #3
When Lizzie asks why the boys and girls can't play together, she finds herself the new captain of the soccer team.

☐ *Alecia's Challenge* by Sandra Diersch #32
Thirteen-year-old Alecia has to cope with a new school, a new stepfather, and friends who have suddenly discovered the opposite sex.

Swimming

☐ *Breathing Not Required* by Michele Martin Bossley #4
An eager synchronized swimmer works hard to be chosen for a solo and almost loses her best friend in the process.

☐ *Water Fight!* by Michele Martin Bossley #14
Josie's perfect sister is driving her crazy but when she takes up swimming — Josie's sport — it's too much to take.

☐ *Taking a Dive* by Michele Martin Bossley #19
Josie holds the provincial record for the butterfly, but in this sequel to *Water Fight,* she can't seem to match her own time and might not go on to the nationals.

☐ *Great Lengths* by Sandra Diersch #26
Fourteen-year-old Jessie decides to find out whether the rumours about a new swimmer at her Vancouver club are true.

Track and Field

☐ *Mikayla's Victory* by Cynthia Bates #29
Mikayla must compete against her friend if she wants to represent her school at an important track event.